No Scone Unturned

A Lexy Baker Cozy Mystery

Leighann Dobbs

This is a work of fiction.

None of it is real. All names, places, and events are products of the author's imagination. Any resemblance to real names, places, or events are purely coincidental, and should not be construed as being real.

One

Lexy Baker stood back, tilted her head, and examined the triple-tiered server on which she'd just laid out two dozen freshly baked scones as the scents of orange, vanilla, and apples wafted up from the still-warm confections to mingle with the earthy aroma of coffee that drifted out from her grandmother's kitchen.

A surge of pride bubbled up as Lexy studied her handiwork. She nibbled the corner of an apple-cinnamon scone, relishing the sweet, doughy taste. Not too sweet and not too spicy. Just enough to tickle the taste buds. Not only were the scones delicious, but the display sitting atop her grandmother's mahogany dining room table looked lovely, too.

She bent down so that the display was at eye level. She reached to adjust the scones, which rested on layers of thick paper doilies, so that they lined up evenly. On the bottom tier, she'd placed cranberry orange on one side with lemon poppy seed on the other. In the middle, she alternated cinnamon apple with maple glazed. The top tier she loaded up with her specialty—ham and cheese.

Even though the display wouldn't be seen by any of her customers, Lexy couldn't help but fuss over the presentation. She wanted her pastries to look as delicious as they tasted. That pride and attention to detail had enabled her to grow her bakery, *the Cup and Cake*, to be one of the most popular in the area.

The scones were test recipes for a brunch catering job she'd landed at the home of one of Brook Ridge Falls' more affluent citizens, Caspian Kingsley. This was her first foray into catering an entire event and not just the desserts. She wanted everything to be perfect and for the baked goods to be especially delicious. The better things tasted, the more guests who attended the event would be enticed to visit her bakery later on and become regular customers.

The taste testers included her grandmother Mona Baker—whom Lexy called Nans—and Nans' three friends, Ida, Ruth, and Helen. The four senior citizens were presently huddled around an open window in Nans' living room, their blue-gray heads bent together, totally ignoring the golden-brown treats on the table.

"The scones are ready for you to taste," Lexy called out, her brows tugging together as she glanced anxiously at the four women. They delighted in taste testing for Lexy and normally would already be seated at the table, their delicate china teacups steaming with coffee and napkins tucked into the tops of their polyester shirts.

"We'll be there in a minute, dear." Nans waved her hand behind her back as if to shoo Lexy away. "We're just playing with Ida's new toy."

"It's not a toy, Mona. It's an expensive piece of equipment, and if my grandson finds out I'm doing this, I'll be in big trouble. So I gotta be careful," Ida said with some degree of consternation, which was strange, since near as Lexy could tell, Ida's middle name was Trouble. The woman seemed to thrive on it.

Helen pushed the window up even farther, letting in a blast of warm summer air. "Come on, Ida, don't be a wuss. Let her rip!"

What are they doing?

Lexy stepped closer to look over Nans' shoulder. Ida held a strange-looking disk with four legs in one hand. It had helicopter-like blades on all four corners and a tiny camera lens on the front. In her other hand she held some sort of controller with an antenna on top, two joystick-like knobs, and a viewing screen.

"What *is* that?" Lexy asked.

"It's a drone. Some quad-copter thingy. My grandson Jason has it for his real estate business, and I ... umm ... borrowed it." Ida glanced at Lexy and winked. "Sort of."

"Does he know you have it?" Helen asked.

"He knows I *have* it. But he doesn't know I'm going to *fly* it."

"You didn't tell him that you *weren't* going to fly it though, did you?" Ruth asked.

"Well, not exactly. He asked me not to, and I pretended I didn't hear him. He thinks I'm deaf."

"Perfect then. We'll just send it for a little spin. Technically you didn't lie to him, and he'll never know, anyway." Nans took the drone from Ida, placed it on her palm, and shoved her hand out the second-story window. "Ready?"

"Hold on now, don't drop it!" Ida clutched the controller, her wrinkled fingers fiddling with one of the knobs.

The blades whirred into action, and the drone hovered an inch off of Nans' palm.

"It's flying!"

Ida twisted the knob, and it shot forward, careening to the left almost sideways. "Oh, crap!"

She jerked the knob in the opposite direction, and the drone overcorrected, careening to the right. "Poo!"

She turned the knob, more gently this time, and it righted itself then glided forward.

"You got it! Now fly it over the complex. Let's see who's out," Ruth said.

Ida gently pushed the middle knob forward, and the drone moved away. As the drone got farther away, Lexy's gaze switched to the LCD display on the transmitter, which showed a bird's-eye view of the Brook Ridge Retirement community as it flew from Nans' apartment through the large complex.

"Look, there's Glenda Willow's house." Ruth tapped the screen.

"And the Millers'," Helen added.

Below, they could see Vera Gorham walking down the sidewalk in a navy-blue T-shirt and white pants. She hesitated, squinting into the sky toward the drone.

"Let's spook Vera. Fly lower!" Nans chuckled.

Ida pressed the controller, and the drone zoomed down toward Vera.

"Whoops, didn't mean to make it go that low." Ida fiddled with the joysticks, and the drone turned around and buzzed Vera from the other direction, barely missing her and ruffling the top of her beehive hairdo.

"Yeeha!" Ruth yelled as they watched Vera raise her arms to swat at the drone, nearly catching its leg in the process.

"Shoot, I can't let her break it!" Ida twisted the joystick, bringing the drone higher so it couldn't be damaged. "Phew. I'd be in deep doo-doo if this thing got busted. Jason paid a lot for it and even got a booster for long range too."

"How far can it go?" Lexy asked.

"Couple miles, I think."

"Let's fly it over to Castle Heights and check out the Kingsleys'," Ruth suggested. "Lexy can get a sneak peek of the yard where she's going to be setting up the catering job, and then when she goes there to talk to Kingsley in person, she can be prepared with ideas."

"Yeah, plus I wanna get an up-close view of how the other half lives," Helen said.

Lexy watched the display panel as Ida wrenched the controls, sending the drone higher, then jerking to the left, then twisting around awkwardly as it followed the parking lot out onto the main road then toward the more affluent section two streets over.

"Jeepers, Ida, you better take flying lessons," Ruth chided. They stood there, all eyes glued to

7

the screen, as they watched the drone fly just above the thickly leafed oak trees, its display showing the multiangled roofs of the large, up-scale older homes. Castle Heights was an affluent section of town that Lexy thought of as moderately rich. Lots of old money lived there, but it wasn't gigantic-estate territory. The neighborhood dated back to the turn of the century, and the homes were stately but not enormous. The lots weren't huge, either, consisting of maybe a half acre or acre, so residents of each house could actually see their neighbors.

"There it is right there." Nans pointed to a brick home with a front courtyard. "You'd set up in back, I guess, right, Lexy?"

"Yep." Lexy watched, mesmerized, as the drone descended then zipped around the side of the house to reveal a lush backyard with perfectly manicured shrubs and colorful splashes of flowers along the perimeter. The yard sloped down to-ward the neighbors', and Lexy tried to pick out an even patch of ground where she would put the tent.

"What's over there?" Lexy tapped the side of the screen, wanting to see if the other section of yard would be more appropriate for a tent. Given the size of the house, the yard was a bit of a disappointment. It wasn't very large, and most of it seemed to be on a slope.

Ida turned the drone around as instructed to reveal a swampy incline that dipped precariously toward a murky pond.

"Yech," Nans said. "Is that the neighbors' pond? What's the house look like?"

Ida zoomed the drone around to reveal the back of an older home whose size was just short of mansion. It was three stories, but the ground dropped off in the back, making the basement a full walk-out and giving it the height of a full four stories from basement to third floor. It was intricately designed, complete with turrets and narrow porches off several of the rooms on the various floors, but the paint was peeling in spots, and the roof shingles were worn.

On the bottom level, large sliding-glass doors opened to a cement patio that housed an outdoor kitchen and unkempt landscaping, all leading to the murky, overgrown pond. Slightly uphill from the pond, it appeared a gazebo was being built. The area was strewn with odd pieces of lumber partially covered by a blue tarp. The gazebo was half constructed—two walls with latticework corners stood at right angles, propping each other up —but the rest of it was in pieces, and the foundation looked only partially poured.

Then the dog opened his mouth, revealing gigantic pointed teeth that crunched down on the drone just before the screen went black.

Two

"What's happened to my drone?" Ida thrust the joysticks back and forth.

She pounded the screen.

She pushed the middle control as far as it would go, but it was no use. The screen remained dark.

"I can't control it. That dog ate it!"

"Dagnab it! We've got to get that drone!" Ruth said.

"Yeah, my grandson is going to kill me," Ida added.

"Your grandson?" Nans fisted her hands on her hips. "I hardly think that's the most important thing. That drone holds the video that can prove we just witnessed a murder!"

"That's right! We need to call the police!" Helen lunged for the vintage turquoise princess phone Nans kept for her landline.

"Call them? Why do that when we have a direct line to Jack?" Ruth pointed at Lexy.

"Right, well ..." Lexy glanced at her cell phone. She had an agreement with her husband, Jack, a homicide detective in the Brook Ridge Police Department. No phone calls during working hours unless it was an emergency.

Is this an emergency? Someone appeared to be dead, after all, but the circumstances under which they'd witnessed it were a little iffy. Besides, wouldn't a neighbor—*or someone*—have seen the body and already called the police?

Even though Nans and the ladies ran a private investigator service—the Brook Ridge Falls Ladies Detective Club—and they sometimes *did* help Jack on cases, he usually took a dim view of them butting into his police work uninvited. And Lexy was *sure* that Nans was already planning on doing some butting in where this case was concerned.

If there even *was* a case. Maybe the woman wasn't dead? Though she sure had looked it. And there was no doubt she had been pushed.

"I could text him," Lexy offered.

"That won't do. Besides, I think we need to see him face to face. This is an urgent matter. A killer could be getting away with murder! We need to get down to the police station right away." Nans' eyes flicked over to the scones piled up on the dining room table. "We'll just pack some of those up to go."

The ladies bustled over to the table. Taking the large embossed napkins from their place settings, they unfolded them and laid them flat on the table. Then each of them picked out a scone, set it in the napkin, folded it back up, and shoved the whole thing into her giant patent-leather purse. The whole process only took a couple of seconds. They'd had lots of experience.

Nans rushed to the door, turned, and looked inquisitively at Lexy. "Well, are you going to drive us or not?"

"Yeah, come on, Lexy." Ruth grabbed her elbow. "We'll give you our verdict on the scones on the way over."

Lexy grabbed her keys with a sigh and followed them out to the parking lot, where they somehow managed to pack themselves into her VW Beetle. The rustle of napkins serenaded her from the back seat.

"These are good, Lexy," Nans mumbled beside her, the napkin spread on her lap.

"I got the cranberry orange. It needs a little bit more orange, I think, dear," Ida said.

"You need to come up with a chocolate scone," Helen said. Then she added apologetically, "Though this apple-cinnamon one is delicious."

"She could've put a little bit more of the granulated sugar on top, don't you think?" Ruth asked.

She pulled into the police station, and Nans, Ruth, Ida, and Helen hopped out, practically running to the door. Lexy followed at a slower pace, feeling a niggle of trepidation about Jack's reaction. Hopefully he would be happy to have witnesses to a case and not wary about Nans and the gang butting in to try and solve it themselves. Which Lexy was sure they would do.

The Brook Ridge police station was a utilitarian brick building that had been in town since the early part of the twentieth century. The lobby had been updated in bland vanilla industrial. It had a row of orange plastic chairs to the left of the entrance and a receptionist desk across from it. It smelled of paperwork and pastrami sandwiches.

The ladies had already breezed past the receptionist and were making a beeline for Jack's office by the time Lexy got inside. They hovered in his doorway, casting glances back at Lexy as she approached. They parted when she got to his door as if her presence was going to get him to take them more seriously.

Jack sat at his desk, his left brow quirked up, his eyes drifting from Nans to Ruth to Ida to Helen and then coming to rest on Lexy.

Lexy quirked her lips in something that she hoped looked like a smile but really felt like a grimace. "Hi."

"What a pleasant surprise," Jack said tentatively then pushed up from his desk and came around to give Lexy a quick peck on the cheek. He took her hand and squeezed it then gestured for Nans, Ruth, Ida, and Helen to fight over the two available chairs. Ida and Ruth won, so Nans and Helen leaned against the wall. Judging by the way Nans tapped her foot impatiently, Lexy figured she couldn't wait to get down to business.

Jack dropped Lexy's hand and leaned his hip on the corner of the green metal desk as he studied them, a hint of amusement in his honey-brown eyes. "Okay, I know this isn't just a social call. What's going on?"

"We've witnessed a murder!" Nans blurted out.

Jack's face turned serious. He glanced back at his computer. "Really? I didn't get any calls about a murder. Are you sure?"

"The body probably hasn't been discovered yet," Ruth said.

Jack's eyes narrowed. "But if you saw it happen, wouldn't you have stayed and called the police? You know better than to leave the scene of a crime."

Nans shuffled her feet. "Well, we weren't *actually* there."

Jack crossed his arms over his chest. "I see. This is one of those hunches, right?" He glanced at Lexy for confirmation.

"No, we *saw* it. It's just … well, it's complicated," Lexy said.

"Why don't you back up and tell me exactly how, when, and where this happened," Jack suggested. At least he wasn't dismissing them right away.

Nans leaned forward. She was in full-on detective persona, her voice taking on an official tone. "Well, you see, Ida had a drone from her grandson Jason, and we were flying it around the neighborhood."

Jack held up his palm. "Wait a minute. A drone?"

"Yeah, you know, one of those things they use to take videos of real estate," Ida cut in. "Jason's a big real estate developer, as you might remember."

"Yes, I remember. Okay, go on, then. You were flying this drone…"

Nans continued. "We were checking out the Kingsleys', where Lexy is going to be doing that big catering job on Wednesday, except Ida didn't really know how to work the controls."

Ida frowned at Nans. "I was working them pretty darn good."

Nans shot a wrinkle-browed look at Ida. "The thing was jerking all over the place, and you were going in the wrong direction."

"You practically ruined Vera's hairdo," Ruth added.

Ida stood facing Ruth and Nans, her hands on her hips. "Well, it was my first time, and I was just getting—"

"Ladies!" Jack cut in, and everyone turned to look at him. "Let's get back to the murder."

Ida sat down, and Nans continued with the story.

"So anyway. It just so happens that writer lady lives right behind the Kingsleys'. Olive Pendleton?" Nans paused to see if Jack recognized the name. He nodded, so she continued. "We wanted to get a gander at her house, and there she was out on a balcony up on the very top floor."

"Tell him the important part," Ida cut in. "She was trying to get a dog off the roof."

"A dog on the roof?" Jack's gaze shifted to Lexy, his right brow quirked up as if seeking confirmation. Lexy nodded, and his eyes flicked back to Nans.

"What was a dog doing on the roof?" he asked.

Nans shrugged. "How should I know? She has a pack of them. Little fluffy things. I don't know what they are."

"Peekapoos," Ruth informed them. When everyone looked at her strangely, she just shrugged and said, "My sister-in-law has one. They're a mix between a Pekingese and a poodle."

"Anyway, one was on the roof, and the woman was leaning out to get it," Nans said.

"And she fell?" Jack went to the other side of his desk and looked at his computer screen. "There would be an ambulance call..."

"Oh no, she didn't fall." Nans leaned toward Jack and paused dramatically. "She was pushed... well, hit over the head, actually."

Jack looked up sharply. "You saw someone hit her over the head. Can you describe them?"

Everyone glanced at each other nervously.

"Not exactly. We didn't see all of him," Ruth said.

"What do you mean?"

"We were watching on the LCD screen of the controller." Helen glanced at Ida apologetically. "It was a little hard to see since the drone wasn't flying so smoothly, and things were a little blurry. But a hand came out from the window and clobbered her on the head with a baseball bat!"

Ida straightened in her chair, shooting a sideways glance at Helen. "We could see good enough, but only his arm was visible."

"That's right," Nans said. "The arm came out, and she was leaning over the balcony to get the dog. He bonked her on the head, and then she fell. It's four stories in the back of that house. She smashed onto the cement patio. Lights out."

"Are you sure it was Olive Pendleton?" Jack asked. "There are no calls from that part of town."

"Absolutely." Ruth nodded vigorously. "She had the blond hair and had on the same maroon sweater she wore for her author photo on the back of her book *Blood on the Forge*."

"You read her books?" Nans asked.

Ruth shrugged. "I read lots of books."

"And you're sure she was dead?" Jack narrowed his eyes at them before looking at his computer screen again.

Ruth nodded. "As a doornail."

"She never moved after that," Nans confirmed.

Jack frowned at his screen. "When was this? I don't have any calls about anyone falling to their death."

The ladies exchanged a glance. "It was about forty-five minutes ago. Surely someone would have found the body by now."

"Yeah, the murderer. Probably trying to make it look like an accident." Ida rummaged in her purse, took out the napkin, unfolded it, and broke off a small piece of scone. "My money's on the husband."

"Well, of course it is," Ruth said. "It usually is the spouse."

"Do you think he was having an affair?" Helen asked.

"Ladies, ladies." Jack sat in the chair, his fingers clicking the keys. "Let's not speculate. That's a job for the police, right? But I don't see any call here. Are you sure you saw this happen? Maybe I should take a look at this video from the drone."

Silence.

Jack's eyes narrowed. "Surely you have this incriminating video, right?"

"That's the other thing." Ida pinched the crumbs from her napkin between her fingers and thumb, then tilted her head back and dropped them into her mouth. "I'd like to report a missing drone."

"Wait. So you don't even have the drone?" Jack asked.

"Well, I got a little nervous when we saw her fall, and my hands were a bit jittery on the controls. The drone swooped down toward the ground. I couldn't pull it up in time, and the dogs came chasing after it. The last thing I saw from the transmitter screen was the inside of a Peekapoo's mouth."

"The dog took it?"

Ida grimaced. "Yeah, and I really need it back or I'm gonna be in dutch with my grandson."

"Not to mention that it has the murder video on it," Nans added. "It's probably lying out in the yard somewhere, so if you simply go over there and retrieve it, we can have this case wrapped up in a jiff."

Jack gestured toward the computer screen. "What case? There's no police call. Which means there's no body. And where there's no body, there's no investigation."

Nans' brows tugged together, her eyes flicking from the back of the monitor to Jack. "But we just told you we witnessed it. Don't you believe us?"

Jack sighed. "It's not that I don't believe you. It's just that without probable cause, I can't go launching an investigation."

"Well, you'd think our say-so would be enough to go on," Ruth huffed.

Jack leaned back in his chair and steepled his fingers. "So let me get this straight. You have no body, no motive, and the dog ate your evidence. And you expect me to convince my boss to launch an investigation?"

"Well, since you put it that way, I guess it would be kind of hard to convince your boss. But we can't just let a killer get away with murder!" Nans said.

Jack rose from his chair, herding them toward the door. "I'll keep my eyes peeled today and see what comes in. Maybe I'll have one of the patrol cars do a drive-by and see what's going on. Unfortunately my hands are tied."

He pushed them out into the hallway, and Ida turned to look at him. "But what about the drone? I want to report that missing!"

"That's just for people, Ida." Nans said.

"Okay, then I want to report it stolen!" Ida said.

"Well, technically it wasn't stolen, but if you want to file a report..." Jack gestured toward the bullpen, where two uniformed officers sat.

"Never mind that." Nans took Ida's elbow and started down the hall. "That will take up too much time for nothing. *We'll* find the drone. Don't worry."

"Mona." Jack's stern tone stopped Nans in her tracks. She turned to look at him. "Don't go investigating this on your own, now."

"Oh, I wouldn't dream of it." Nans waved a hand in the air and turned around.

Jack leaned against the doorframe, his arms crossed over his chest. He looked down at Lexy. "She's gonna investigate, isn't she?"

Lexy watched the backs of the ladies as they marched down the hall. "'Fraid so."

Jack sighed and stepped back into his office. "Okay, all I can say is ... just be careful. Judging by what you saw, there may be a clever killer on the loose, and he's not going to like four nosey old ladies and one cute baker digging into his business."

Three

"Was Jack mad?" Nans asked after they were all situated in the car.

"No. He seemed...resigned." A smile played on Lexy's lips as she thought about how far Jack had come with regard to her investigating murder cases.

Nans and Jack had been neighbors, and she'd initially met him when she'd bought Nans' house —the one she and Jack lived in now. Of course, there had been that unfortunate incident in which *she* was suspected of murder that had thrown her and Jack together. But Nans had been thinking about fixing them up for months, though Lexy wasn't sure if that was because she thought Jack and Lexy would be good together or if she just wanted to get closer to him so she could get in on more investigations. Either way, things had worked out pretty well for Nans—and Lexy—on both counts.

At first, Jack hadn't been keen on either Nans or Lexy investigating. In fact, he'd been downright resistant. And while Lexy loved running *the Cup and Cake*, she must have inherited some of the investigating gene from her grandmother, because she couldn't resist digging into murders. It had been a bone of contention between her and Jack in the beginning, but now he was really coming around. Sometimes he even fed them clues on the side. Hopefully, this would be one of those times. She had a feeling they were going to need his help.

"Well then, if he's *resigned*, we might as well take a ride over to the Pendleton house and see what we can see." Nans slid her eyes over to Lexy.

"I really should be getting to the bakery..." The dejected sighs from the ladies in the back seat gave Lexy pause. "But since Cassie is there now, I guess I could take a quick swing over. Maybe I can get a better look at the Kingsley property in person."

"That's my girl!" Nans patted her knee.

"Hopefully that drone is just lying out in the yard somewhere, and I can grab it," Ida said.

"I don't know." Images of Sprinkles taking her favorite toys and hiding them sprang to mind.

"Sprinkles likes to hide her toys. We may have to do some hunting."

Ruth rubbed her hands together. "Good. I'd love getting my hands dirty."

"Maybe we can find the murder weapon," Helen said. "He might keep it beside the door or in the garage."

The Pendleton house was on a quiet street lined with tall maple trees. Birds twittered and chirped in the leaves overhead while chipmunks darted in and out of an old stone wall at the edge of the property. Lexy had parked on the intersecting street, thinking they could walk to the Pendletons' and then backtrack past the car and over to the next street to get a look at the Kingsleys' yard in person.

As they strolled toward the Pendletons', Ida grabbed Nans arm and pulled her back. "Look! You can see the backyard from here," she whispered, pointing to a space in between the shrubs that revealed a section of the patio and the half-finished gazebo.

Nans parted the shrubs and poked her face through, craning her neck to see. She turned and looked at them over her shoulder. "I don't see any dead body there," she whispered.

"And apparently one hasn't been discovered." Ruth gestured to the quiet street. "There are no police cars, no commotion. Look, there's not even any crime-scene tape."

Nans pulled her head out of the shrub and looked around, her forehead creasing. "You're right. That's odd. Where is the body?"

"You don't think she could have survived, do you?" Helen asked.

"I don't think *anyone* could survive that fall. You saw her lying there. And the blood..." Nans shuddered. "But even if by some miracle she did survive, she would've surely needed a trip to the hospital, and Jack said there was no such emergency call."

"Well, maybe that happened in between the time we left Jack's office and arrived here," Ruth suggested.

Nans pressed her lips together. "Doubtful. But there's one way to find out." She clutched her purse tighter and marched toward the Pendleton house.

The house didn't look quite as dilapidated from the front as it had from the back. It was an English Tudor design with eyebrow windows and lightning rod–topped turrets. The front steps led to an old oak door made for giants and rounded at the top, with big iron hinges turned black with age. The windows had diamond-shaped grilles, giving the house the look of an oversized cottage.

Nans marched toward the door, her sensible beige shoes squeaking on the slate slabs that made up the walkway.

"Hold up there, Mona." Ida crouched to look under an azalea bush, brushing away a pile of crisp dead leaves that had accumulated underneath. "That drone could be anywhere." She darted over to a giant rhododendron, pulling apart the branches and peering in.

But Nans was already knocking on the front door. Lexy heard a chorus of barking, and then the door opened, revealing a man in his mid-sixties. His salt-and-pepper hair was cut short and covered only the sides of his head. The top was shiny and bald. He was wearing a white T-shirt and an angry scowl. Four dogs circled the mud-stained cuffs of his tan chinos, and Lexy was relieved to see one of them was the black dog that had been on the roof.

He looked Nans up and down with narrowed eyes. Then his gaze drifted over her shoulder to assess the rest of them. "I told you ladies before. We don't like fans coming to the house unannounced." He started to close the door.

Nans stuck her foot in the door. "Hey, we're not fans. We've come to see Olive."

The man stopped long enough to stare inquisitively at her. "Aren't you the ladies from that fan club that's been hanging around here?"

Nans shook her head. "No."

Something to their right caught his attention, and his eyes jerked in that direction, where Ida was on her hands and knees rummaging through a forsythia bush.

"*What* is that woman doing over there?" he demanded.

Nans' head whipped around. "Ida, stop that!" She turned back to the man and whispered, "Sorry, she's a little bit senile. That's why we've come, you see. My poor friend here, well, she doesn't have long, and she'd really like to see a famous author in person."

The man didn't seem at all sympathetic to Nans' story about Ida. He glanced back into the house over his shoulder uncertainly. "My wife is... napping."

"Suuure she is." Ida, who had joined them, brushed the dirt from the knees of her tan polyester slacks.

"I'm sorry, but she works very hard and needs to rest. Maybe you could make an appointment on her website like normal people. We don't like strangers just showing up here." And then he slammed the door in their faces.

"Well, go figure that," Ruth said as they turned from the door and started down the walk. "Sounds to me like he was a little bit upset that we were asking for Olive."

"Well, he couldn't very well have her come to the door." Helen leaned toward them and lowered her voice. "Because she's dead."

"Now where do you think those dogs would have hidden that drone?" Ida stood on the sidewalk several feet down from the house. She rose on her tiptoes and looked over a tall hedge, trying to see into the backyard. She tsked and shook her head then bent and moved a large rock aside with a grunt.

"Never mind the drone," Nans said. "Where did he hide the *body*?"

"Not to mention the murder weapon," Helen said.

"Why hide the body at all?" Ruth asked.

"If there even is a body," Lexy said.

"If she'd survived the fall, then he would've been at the hospital with her, not answering the door and pretending she was napping inside," Helen pointed out.

Ida picked up the edge of another rock, looked under it, and then squealed and dropped it when it revealed a large, brownish-red, wriggling centipede.

"Stop it, Ida. The dog didn't put your drone under a rock," Ruth said.

"Well, it's not lying around in the yard. At least not that I can see. We might need to make a midnight reconnaissance mission out here." Ida's blue eyes sparkled.

"That might not be a bad idea on a few counts," Helen said. "This case is starting to look mighty strange, and it wouldn't hurt for us to poke around for some evidence."

"True. I don't know if they have a security system, though." Nans turned around and scanned the house and perimeter of the yard. "You have to wonder...if Olive is dead, then why doesn't her husband want her body to be found? He must have a very unusual motive." Nans stopped short before tripping over Ida, who had stopped to poke around under another shrub, pushing stones out of the way. "Come on, Ida, we don't have time for this. We've got to get back to my place and do some research."

"But the drone! Jason will be looking for it soon, and I—"

"Don't worry, Ida. We'll find it. I promise you, we'll leave no stone unturned in our search to prove there was a murder here ... and that drone is a key piece of evidence."

Four

Lexy spent the rest of the day at *the Cup and Cake.* Her bakery was on Brook Ridge Falls' Main Street overlooking the waterfall the town was named for. She was happiest when she was in the kitchen baking...except maybe when she could be looking into a mysterious murder.

But she had a business to run, so she experimented with the scone recipe, adding a little more sugar to the tops, more orange zest to the cranberry-orange recipe, and she even came up with a chocolate scone to add to her offerings.

It was a slow afternoon and not many customers came, so when five o'clock rolled around, she already had the café tables by the windows cleaned, the self-serve coffee station emptied and ready for tomorrow's brew, and the glass cases that displayed her pastries scrubbed free of fingerprints.

She drove home, wondering if Jack had received any calls about Olive Pendleton. Maybe Olive's husband had needed time to stage the body to incriminate someone else before calling the police. If he had, would Jack have texted her?

Jack was already there when she got to the old Craftsman-style bungalow she'd bought when Nans had moved into the retirement community. The home held a lot of warm memories from her childhood, and now she and Jack were making even more memories there.

"Woof!"

A ball of white fur hurled itself across the living room into Lexy's arms. A warm tongue lapped at her face.

"Okay, Sprinkles, okay." Lexy put the dog down and stroked her silky fur. She was rewarded with a happy gaze of adoration from the dog's brown eyes that warmed her heart. "I guess someone's happy to see me."

"That makes two of us." Jack had come in from the kitchen and was standing next to her. Lexy gazed up into his brown eyes, and her stomach fluttered as he opened his arms. They'd been married for a couple of years now, but her heart still beat a little faster when she was near him. She eagerly slipped into his embrace and accepted his kiss. She'd been half worried he might be mad about her visit to the police station, but his kiss told her he wasn't holding any grudges.

"I put some steaks on the grill and was just making a salad." Jack gestured toward the kitchen. Lexy tossed her purse onto the couch and followed Jack into the kitchen with Sprinkles trotting at her heels.

Lexy had kept the kitchen pretty much the same as it had been when Nans owned the house. Black and white linoleum floor and crisp, white-painted cabinets. A pile of grape tomatoes sat on a cutting board on the counter. Lexy pushed Jack toward the back door. She appreciated that he started supper when he got home first but didn't think he needed to do all the work. "I'll finish the salad. You check the steaks."

The mouthwatering smell of grilled meat wafted in through the back door as Jack opened it. Lexy focused on slicing the small tomatoes in half, popping a few of them into her mouth. They were no substitute for Jack's perfectly seared steaks.

He came back in, slipped an arm around her waist, and nuzzled her neck. "They're almost done. How's the salad coming?"

"Pretty much done." She nestled into his embrace just as Sprinkles trotted in with a stuffed penguin in her mouth. She pushed in between Lexy and Jack, oblivious to the fact that she was intruding on their moment. When Lexy didn't respond, the dog jumped on her leg.

"Do you have a new toy?" Lexy looked up at Jack, who nodded.

"I had some extra time after work, and her old one was falling apart," he said.

Lexy crouched and tugged on one end of the toy. Sprinkles tugged back and let out a friendly growl. Lexy tugged harder. Sprinkles let go, and Lexy tossed the toy across the kitchen.

Sprinkles scrambled across the linoleum, her claws sliding on the slick surface as she skidded over to retrieve the toy and bring it back to Lexy. Lexy tossed it again, and Sprinkles went through the same routine, except this time, instead of bringing the toy back, she trotted off to the living room with it in her mouth.

"Looks like she won't even bring a new toy back more than once." No matter how many times Lexy had tried, she could not get Sprinkles to fetch more than once. Instead, she'd run off and hide the toy. Lexy thought about the Pendletons' Peekapoos. Did they run off and hide their toys, even if one of them was a drone? Lexy peered out into the living room to see Sprinkles shoving the toy under the couch—one of her favorite hiding spots.

Lexy turned her attention back to Jack, who was gathering a handful of plates, utensils, and condiments so they could eat outside.

"You never got a call about Olive Pendleton?" Lexy asked as she covered the salad bowl and followed him out to the patio.

"Nope. Weird, huh?"

"Very." Lexy chewed her bottom lip, wondering if Jack would say any more about it. Should she ask? Usually it was best to wait him out.

The steaks let out one last sizzle as Jack speared them with a large fork and moved them from the grill to a platter. He set the platter on the table, and they got busy loading up their plates and eating.

After a few bites, Jack finally said, "I did do a little bit of research, though."

Lexy's brows shot up. "Oh really? So you do believe us."

"Of course I believe you. I waited all day for a call to come in, but nothing ever came. I'm limited as to what I can do officially." Jack swallowed a piece of steak and washed it down with some red wine. "I assume you guys did some investigating after you left my office."

"You know how Nans is. But we didn't do anything bad. We just went over to the Pendletons'. Naturally the body was no longer there, and when we knocked on the door, the husband said Olive was napping."

"Maybe the fall wasn't as bad as you thought?" Jack suggested. "Helen said the video was a little hard to see. Maybe she did fall but didn't need medical attention."

"No way. She fell four stories, and there was blood. Lots of it." Lexy shivered and pushed her food away, remembering the sight of Olive Pendleton smashed on the cement slab. "What I don't get is why. I mean, I could see him clubbing her on the head so she'd fall, and then he could say it was an accident. The part I don't get is the husband pretending she's still alive."

Jack shrugged. "Maybe he's not the killer. Maybe whoever the killer is lives in that house or has access to it and told the husband Olive was sleeping."

"And he didn't notice? Why would the killer want to hide the body, and what did they do with it?"

Jack leaned back and sipped his wine. "Good questions. I don't know the answers. I can see something fishy is going on, but I can't investigate officially. However, I did manage to dig up something that might help *you*."

Lexy felt a surge of excitement. "Really? What?"

"Well, I don't know if I should tell you. Maybe we could barter for it," Jack said suggestively.

Lexy's lips curled in a smile. She leaned across, accepting the hand he held out to her. "I'm up for a little bartering."

"Okay. This may not be anything, but I had Wendy do a little research in her downtime. We didn't have anything in the police database, but she did run across a strange court case in which Olive tried to sue her parents about changes in their will."

Lexy's brows drew together. "Can you do that?"

"No. It was thrown out, but the record is still there."

"So what happened?"

"It seems her family—her maiden name was McMurty—was wealthy, but they didn't approve of Olive's career choice or of her husband, Rupert," Jack said.

Picturing Rupert with his stained pants and scowl, Lexy could see why. "They didn't like that she was an author?"

"Nope. They were afraid she'd die a starving artist, and they said Rupert would spend the money like it was burning a hole in his pocket."

"But she's successful and has a big house..." Lexy's voice drifted off as she pictured the peeling paint and unkempt lawn. Was Olive broke or just eccentric?

"They died about ten years ago, probably before her books became famous. Anyway, they had a codicil in the will that prohibited Rupert from getting any of the McMurty money. Olive made quite a ruckus about it when her mom told her. There was a domestic call about that, and Olive had to be taken into custody. Sounds like she had a bit of a temper."

"So if Olive died, Rupert wouldn't get anything she'd inherited from her parents..." That wasn't a very good reason to kill her, but it was a good reason to pretend she was still alive...*except* Olive was a famous author, so she probably had plenty of her own money that Rupert would inherit. It didn't make sense for him to take such a big chance on killing her and then pretend she was alive just to get her parents' money. "How much did she inherit?"

"I don't know. I know she has a sister and they split the money, but it was almost a decade ago. For all I know, she already spent it. Ruth might be able to work her magic online and find out."

"Still doesn't make much sense. If she inherited a decade ago, why would Rupert wait until now to kill her? And if she had money, why was their house in such disrepair?"

"I don't know about the money, but according to what Wendy said, Olive had all her books in a literary trust, and her parents made a big stink about that, too."

"Stink?"

"Yep. They must have really hated Rupert, because they put a codicil in their will that would make her sister sole trustee of the McMurty family trust if Olive named Rupert as beneficiary to her literary trust. That means her sister would control all the McMurty family money."

"Huh. So what did she do?"

"She listed her dogs as the beneficiaries of her trust."

"Her dogs? So that means if Olive died, Rupert wouldn't get any of the money from her books?"

Jack nodded. "That's right."

"Well, that sounds like a motive to kill her and pretend she was still alive to me."

Five

Lexy couldn't wait to tell Nans what Jack had found out about the McMurty will the next day. Not to mention that Jack had practically given them the green light to investigate. She suffered through the morning rush at *the Cup and Cake,* handing out doughnuts and her famous cupcake tops. She even made a batch of chocolate scones, which were a big hit with the morning crowd. Apparently Helen wasn't the only one with a hankering for chocolate scones.

When her assistant, Cassie, arrived to relieve her, Lexy eagerly hung up her vintage cherry-pattern apron, shoved some chocolate and cranberry-orange scones into a white bakery box, and ran out the door.

Nans and the others were already seated around the dining room table in Nans' apartment, their iPads out in front of them and the scones from the day before in the center of the table.

Lexy noticed the pastry server was half empty. The ladies had been busy.

They didn't waste time on formalities, either. As soon as Nans opened the door, she pulled Lexy into the apartment and shoved her into a chair. Ida relieved her of the bakery box, lifting the lid an inch to peek inside then nodding her approval before transferring the scones to the serving tray.

"Chocolate!" Helen squealed as she helped herself.

"Coffee?" Nans asked Lexy.

"Please." The *bub-bub-bub* of the old-fashioned percolator in the kitchen and the enticing aroma of the earthy blend of Nans' coffee had Lexy's palms itching to curl around a steaming mug.

Ida leaned across the table toward Lexy. "Okay, enough of the small talk. Spill it. What did you get out of Jack last night?"

The others snickered around mouthfuls of scones.

"Did he get any calls about the case?" Nans slid a mug in front of Lexy then pointed to her living room. "As you can see, we don't have much to go on."

Lexy leaned over to look into the living room. They'd pulled the six-foot-long whiteboard out from the spare room and had already made lines to divide it into sections with headings such as "suspects," "motive," and "clues." Unfortunately, the whiteboard was mostly blank. Apparently they hadn't made much headway.

"I'm not convinced he actually believed us." Ruth broke off part of a ham-and-cheese scone and put it on the dainty china dessert plate in front of her.

"Did anyone find my drone and turn it in?" Ida asked.

"Sorry, Ida, no one found the drone. And Jack *did* believe us, but no calls came in about Olive Pendleton, so there's nothing for him to investigate." Lexy paused, relishing the fact that she had more information than Nans and the ladies did. It was rare that she knew something they didn't. "I did manage to get a little tidbit of information out of him, though."

She took a sip of coffee, knowing the ladies were probably wetting their pants in anticipation. They watched her patiently with tilted heads and inquisitive faces.

"Well, out with it, Lexy!" Nans demanded finally.

"Yeah, we don't have all day," Ida said impatiently. Then added, "This cranberry-orange is much better. New recipe?"

"I tweaked it to add more orange zest."

"It's perfect."

"Can we get a move on? There's a murderer on the loose, in case you guys have forgotten," Helen said. "What did Jack tell you?"

Lexy chose an apple-cinnamon scone from the tray and picked away at it while she told the ladies about Olive Pendleton's parents' will and her literary trust.

"That gives him a perfect motive to pretend she's still alive," Ruth said.

"Right. While she's still alive, he can collect the royalties. If she's dead, he gets nothing," Nans agreed.

"But why *kill* her? Unless he didn't want her around for some reason," Helen said.

"Which means he must be having an affair!" Ida's voice rose with excitement.

Nans jumped up and went to the whiteboard, filling in the new information under the "motive" category. She turned to them with her brows tugged together. "There's just one thing. If Olive has money, then why don't they take care of the house better?"

"Plenty of creative people are eccentric. Maybe she's one of them," Ruth said. "They are building that new gazebo. Maybe they're getting the house redone or something and the work just hasn't started yet."

"We need to find out more about these trusts and their finances." Ruth tapped her iPad, and the screen lit up.

"And who he would be having an affair with," Ida said. "Because if money isn't the motive, then it's got to be love."

"Unless Olive was going to divorce him," Lexy suggested.

Ida snapped her fingers. "That's right! Maybe *Olive* was having the affair!"

"Wouldn't blame her," Ruth said. "He seemed grouchy."

"Yeah, and he doesn't have much going for him in the looks department, either," Helen added.

The whiteboard marker squeaked as Nans jotted down their ideas and Ruth's fingers flew over the surface of the iPad. Nans stood back and crossed her arms, tapping the capped end of the marker on her lips.

"But where did he hide the body?" Nans asked.

"And where is the drone?" Ida added.

"What about the pond?" Helen said.

"The pond *was* rather murky. There could be a body right under the surface, and no one would notice it," Ruth said.

"Or a drone," Ida added.

"It would be easy to drag the body from that cement patio down to the pond," Nans added.

"I noticed the cuffs of his pants had mud on them," Lexy said.

"We need to get in that yard and check out that pond." Ida slid her eyes over to Lexy. "And what better way than through the neighbors' yard?"

"The Kingsleys'? I don't think..." Lexy had a consultation with Caspian Kingsley later that afternoon, but she didn't want the ladies tagging along. That wouldn't be good for business. Somehow when Nans and the ladies were around, something always went wrong.

"Wait a minute." Ruth spoke up before Ida could make the request. Ruth tapped her fingernail on the surface of the iPad. "Olive Pendleton's books are on Amazon. Amazon is the biggest bookseller in the business, you know."

"It stands to reason her books would be on there, then, right?" Nans asked.

"Sure. But here's the thing. Look at her rankings." Ruth turned the iPad around so they could see the screen. "She's ranked way down around five hundred thousand. Her books aren't selling well at all."

They all craned their necks to look.

"Huh. Maybe that explains why their house is in disrepair," Nans said.

"But it wouldn't explain why Rupert would hide her body and pretend she was alive," Ida added.

"Wait a minute." Helen paused with a scone midway to her mouth. "I seem to recall hearing she had a new book coming out. That would spur interest in her other works, wouldn't it?"

"Oh yes, a new release always brings in new interest," Ruth said. "Now let me Google... oh yes, here it is. She does have a new book." Ruth looked at them over the rims of her bright-red reading glasses. "And it's coming out next week."

Nans clapped her hands. "Well, that explains it. If the book is coming out next week, then she's already written it. It's probably in the publishing process right now. Rupert is probably just pretending she's alive so that the checks will keep rolling in and not be channeled elsewhere due to the terms of her trust."

"Maybe he's even going to manufacture some kind of mystery around it. You know, like what happened when Agatha Christie disappeared." Ida's blue eyes sparkled. "That would increase sales, wouldn't it?"

"He could milk this for months, and I bet he'd make more money than ever on those books," Ruth said.

"And with no body and no murder investigation, the police won't be poking around, and he could still continue his affair while collecting all the royalties," Ida said.

"Well, we don't know for sure that he's having an affair," Nans pointed out. "This could all just be about the money."

"Right," Helen said. "We need to check into that."

"How do we do that?" Lexy asked.

"Easy. Every neighborhood has a busybody, right?" Helen looked at Ida. "I bet *you* were the busybody in your neighborhood, Ida. Tell us how we would figure out who the busybody is in the Pendletons' neighborhood."

Ida straightened in her seat and shot Helen a nasty look. Nans and Ruth tried not to laugh.

"Well, I'm not sure exactly, but I think that if you want to find the neighborhood busybody, you have to go check out the neighborhood. They're usually looking out the windows to see what is going on. So all we have to do is go back there and see who's watching." Ida picked up another scone and chomped down on it so hard that Lexy was afraid her dentures would fall out.

Nans clicked the cap on the whiteboard marker. "Luckily, we have a perfect excuse to go back to the neighborhood." Nans turned her gaze on Lexy, and Lexy's stomach dropped. "Lexy, you're meeting with Caspian Kingsley this afternoon to finalize details on your catering job, aren't you?"

"Yes, but I usually go alone, and I don't really think I need—"

"Excellent." Nans cut her off. "What time are you going to pick us up?"

Six

Lexy had tried to get out of taking Nans and the ladies to the Kingsleys', but Nans had nipped her protests in the bud by giving her "the look." The one she'd been giving Lexy since she was a little girl. The one that Lexy couldn't say no to.

So she picked them up at four p.m. and drove over to the Castle Heights neighborhood, parking on the same intersecting street at Ida's request. Ida wanted an opportunity to scan the Pendletons' yard for the drone as they walked down the street.

When they got out of the car, Ruth made it a point to canvass the neighborhood. Lexy thought maybe she was trying to be discreet, but her jagged movements and the way she was craning her neck, whirling around, and peeking over the top of the car made it pretty obvious she was looking for something.

"What are you doing, Ruth?" Nans asked.

"I'm looking for the neighborhood busybody." Ruth zeroed in on something, her eyes narrowing. "And I think I found her."

Across the street was a brick house with black shutters and trumpet vines climbing up the chimney. It wasn't as stately as the others but still bigger than the average house. It sat on a moderately landscaped lot. The window shades were drawn, but in one window they could see two fingers had pried the louvers apart. Someone was looking out at them. As they watched, the louvers snapped shut.

"Well, I think she's on to us," Helen said.

"That's okay. Those types always like to talk. She'll welcome us when we show up at her door." Ruth hitched her purse up on her shoulder and started toward the Kingsleys'.

"*If* we show up at her door." Lexy fell into step behind Ruth. "Now I want you guys to just keep quiet. Don't say anything. I told Kingsley I might be bringing some...err...assistants. You don't need to open your mouths at all." Lexy fixed them with a stern glare. Even though they nodded in agreement, she had a feeling they weren't going to follow her instructions.

The ladies stood silently behind Lexy as she knocked on the Kingsleys' door. The Kingsley house was in much better repair than the Pendletons'. It was almost as large but a more elegant style that dated from the 1920s, with weathered cedar shingles and crisp white trim. The landscaping was not overdone, the shrubs were meticulously trimmed, and there were window boxes on the lower windows, overflowing with purple and white petunias.

The door was answered by Caspian Kingsley, whose personal appearance was as meticulous as that of his house. He wore a crisp blue-and-white pinstriped Oxford shirt and linen slacks. His tanned face radiated a healthy glow and made him look a decade younger than the mid-sixties that Lexy knew him to be.

"Lexy. How lovely to see you again." Caspian held his hand out, and Lexy shook it. His questioning gaze drifted over her shoulder to Nans and the ladies.

"This is my grandmother, Mona Baker, and her friends. They may be assisting me when I cater." Lexy leaned closer to Kingsley and whispered, "They're elderly, with not much excitement in their lives, so I brought them along."

Behind Lexy, the four ladies gasped.

"Well, I would hardly say that we're—" Nans started but snapped her mouth shut when Lexy pinned her with a steely glare. Lexy turned back to Kingsley, unable to help the smile that tugged the corners of her lips. She knew the ladies wouldn't like being portrayed as bored and elderly, but it served them right. She wanted to show them that insisting on tagging along with her came with its drawbacks.

"The venue will be set up out in back." Kingsley turned, indicating for them to follow. They walked through a marble foyer into a lemon-cleaner–scented living room done elegantly in creams and blacks and then out one of the triple sets of French doors to the backyard that they had seen from the street the other day.

"I'll be having a tent set up, and I think this spot will be perfect." Lexy pointed to the one section of yard that was fairly level. Then she turned and pointed at the other side, which sloped down toward the Pendletons'. "And I was thinking about setting up a little bar with mimosas over here, but with this slope, I don't know..." She let her voice trail off as she looked out over the Pendletons' yard. She already knew what she was going to do about the slope, but she wanted to pretend she was thinking so she could have more time to scope out what was going on at the Pendletons'.

Her eyes immediately flew to the cement patio. From this angle, a larger section of patio was visible than she'd been able to see from the street.

Smack dab in the middle was a dark stain. And if she wasn't mistaken, that was exactly where Olive Pendleton had fallen to her death.

"...and I was wondering if we could have some of those cupcake tops." Kingsley's words jerked Lexy's attention back to the real reason she was here.

"Yes. Of course. And quiche and the usual eggs, bacon, sausage, and toast, right?"

"Yes, and I would like some..." His brows drew together as he looked past Lexy's shoulder. "*What* is your grandmother doing?"

Lexy spun around to see Nans, Ruth, Ida, and Helen scrambling down the back of the yard that sloped toward the pond. For a second Lexy thought they might be about to slide in, but they stopped themselves just short of the edge, where a group of cat-o-nine-tails stuck up out of the water.

"That's the neighbors' pond, ladies," Kingsley yelled to them then turned concerned eyes on Lexy. "Are they senile? They won't jump in, will they?"

"I wouldn't put it past them."

Nans waved from the edge of the pond. "Sorry, I dropped something and it rolled down the hill."

Kingsley's lips pursed together. "I do wish the neighbors would clean that yard up."

"Yeah, why don't they? Doesn't the author Olive Pendleton live there?" Lexy asked.

"Yep. They're eccentric. I mean, just look the yard. It needs work. The pond is a mess. Yet they're building a new gazebo, and even that is being done in a slipshod manner. As you can see, they have the walls built but still have yet to finish the footing." Kingsley waved his hand toward the gazebo, where Lexy could see bags of cement lying at the foot of the partially studded wall.

Rupert was actually in the gazebo, apparently working on it, and the voices must have caught his attention. He looked over, his eyes narrowing as he recognized Nans and the ladies.

"Hey, get away from my pond!" He raised his fists in the air and started toward them, but his foot slipped in the mud near the gazebo, and he stopped to right himself. The four Peekapoos, however, had no problem with the mud, and they ran over to the edge of the property, barking and yipping.

Nans and the ladies scrambled up from the embankment.

"Not very friendly, I take it," Lexy said.

"Like I said, they're odd ducks. And those dogs, they make a racket," Kingsley said distastefully.

The ladies had come to join them, and Ruth said, "Must be a lot going on next door with all the women coming and going."

Kingsley gave her a funny look. "Well, I wouldn't say there's a lot of women. Then again, her sister is there a lot. Susan. She always did follow Olive around like a puppy."

"You know her sister?" Nans asked.

Kingsley nodded. "I know the family. Known them for decades. This was the McMurty family home before their parents died. Olive always was the smart one and Susan was the pretty one. She's quite a wallflower despite her beauty—so fragile. You know the type. Delicate. Always sick. Funny how two sisters can be so different. As you can see, Olive is wild with money, but Susan is the opposite. Lives frugally. Doesn't spend it willy-nilly like Olive and Rupert."

"So the two sisters are close, eh?" Ida slid her eyes over to Kingsley. "And Rupert, does he get along with Susan?"

"I assume so. She's here all the time, and they appear to get along. Poor Susan doesn't really have anyone else. Her marriage ended badly. 'Course, Susan always did do everything Olive did. Even got one of those fluffy little dogs. She dotes on that thing, especially since Brent won't have anything to do with her."

"Brent?" Lexy asked.

"Her son. They had a falling out...well, it's really not my place to be airing their laundry."

"And what about the other women?" Helen asked.

"Other women?" Kingsley frowned. "I don't know about any other women. Not too many people go over there unless they have one of their raucous parties." Kingsley glanced disapprovingly at the patio. From this angle, Lexy could see the outdoor kitchen better. It had a stainless steel grill that looked to be in good working order, a giant stainless steel chest that looked like a cooler or freezer, and a large fridge. The stone counters were a little the worse for wear, and the appliances needed polishing but looked to be in good condition otherwise. It also looked well used, but Lexy had a hard time picturing a happy crowd of people holding drinks in their hands and chatting while dour Rupert worked the grill.

Kingsley pressed his lips together thoughtfully. "Oh wait! There is that one woman, I think it's Olive's assistant, or maybe she's the maid, I'm not quite sure. A blonde. Looks similar to Olive and her sister. Quite honestly I don't pay that much attention to what's going on over there. I'm not one of those nosy neighbors like Mrs. Jensen."

"Mrs. Jensen?" Nans said. "She wouldn't happen to live in the brick house with the trumpet vines, would she?"

"Yes, how did you know?" Kingsley asked.

Nans nodded at the ladies knowingly. "Oh, we are very observant."

"So the sister and the maid are usually over there. What about other men? Don't Rupert or Olive have male friends?" Ida asked.

"No, I don't recall any. Like I said, we don't pay much attention to what goes on over there. It's usually just Olive and Rupert."

"So you didn't hear anything strange over there the other day." Nans jerked her chin in the direction of the Pendletons' patio.

"Strange? No. What are you getting on about?" Kingsley's eyes darted from Nans to Lexy. He seemed like he was starting to get suspicious, so Lexy shrugged, pointed to the four ladies, and twirled her finger around her ear to indicate maybe they weren't all there.

Kingsley's eyes turned sympathetic, and he cleared his throat. "Oh, ummm... We try not to pay attention. Too much dog yapping. I only wish our shrubs would grow higher and block them entirely. We hardly come out here anymore."

"Maybe if her books were doing better, they'd have the money to fix the place up," Ruth said.

"Her books?" Kingsley waved his hand, "Pfft. She doesn't need the money from that. She has plenty of money from her folks." Kingsley frowned as he glanced over at Rupert Pendleton, who had gone back to working on the gazebo. "Unless they've already spent it."

"I hope the yapping dogs won't be a problem with the brunch out here," Helen said.

"Me too." Kingsley looked at Lexy. "They can be a bit obnoxious. I have half a mind to call the cops the next time they get on one of their incessant barking jags. Anyway, do you have enough information?"

"Oh, yes. Thank you so much."

"And you'll be here Wednesday morning ready and set up in time for the first guests to arrive at ten a.m.?" Kingsley herded them toward the French doors.

Lexy was about to assure him they would when Nans answered for her. "Oh yes, we will. Don't worry, we'll *all* be here and set up and waiting for your guests with bells on."

As Kingsley led them into the house, Lexy thought she heard him mutter, "I was afraid she was going to say that."

Seven

"You ladies are not invited to the catering event at the Kingsleys'," Lexy whispered as they left the Kingsleys' house.

"Oh, now come on, Lexy, you could use some extra help, couldn't you?" Ruth looked at her with innocent eyes.

"Yes, but somehow I don't think you guys would be much help."

"Now, now. We'll deal with that when it comes," Nans said as they proceeded slowly down the street toward Lexy's car. Ida skirted the edge of the Pendletons' property, her hawklike gaze scouring every inch, looking for her drone. Over at the gazebo, Rupert glared at them, tracking their every move.

The neighborhood was quiet, with no traffic except one Prius that drove slowly past them. The heads of the four senior citizens swiveling toward the Pendletons' property reminded Lexy of Nans and the ladies.

"Did you guys see anything in the pond?" Lexy asked.

Ruth shook her head. "It's as murky as the coffee they have in the senior center. We may have to go in."

Lexy slid her eyes over to Ruth. "Go in?"

"Yeah. You remember when we took those scuba diving lessons last year? I still have my wetsuit, and so does Ida."

"Well, we have to do that at night." Helen gestured toward Rupert. "Hawkeye over there isn't going to let us just jump into his pond if he catches us."

"I'm afraid his alarm system would warn him if we ventured onto the property." Nans pointed to the four dogs, who were now racing across the yard toward them. Apparently they didn't like the way Ida was rummaging in the hedges at the edge of the property.

"*Woof!*"

"*Yap!*"

"*Growl!*"

"Hey, you mangy mutt, let go!"

Lexy looked through the thick shrubbery to see Ida in a pitched battle with the black Peekapoo, who had the corner of her purse in his mouth. Ida was holding the handle, pulling back, while the small dog used his back legs to dig into the ground.

"Come on, Ida, you can't beat a little seven-pound dog?" Nans asked. "I told you you needed to hit the gym more."

Rip!

The dog ripped a piece of shiny patent leather from the corner of Ida's purse, and Ida fell back on her butt. The dogs ran off victoriously toward the patio.

"Dagnab it! I just got this purse at Talbot's!" Ida's face turned sour as she inspected the bottom of the purse, then her eyes flicked out to watch the dogs as they ran to the outdoor kitchen, presumably to hide their new treasure.

"Looks like you got an excuse to get another new purse," Lexy said as Ida stood and brushed off the back of her tan polyester stretch pants before elbowing her way out of the hedge.

"Yeah, but this one's got all nice compartments in it." Ida opened the purse to show her, and Lexy noticed it was filled to the brim with various household objects, lipstick, and even another scone wrapped in a napkin.

"Forget about that." Ruth pointed in the direction of the dogs. "We may have just found one of their hiding spots."

Ida squinted in the direction Ruth was pointing. "You think they hid the drone under that big freezer?"

"I don't know if it would fit," Nans said.

"Maybe they have more than one hiding place," Lexy suggested. "I know Sprinkles has places all over the yard."

"I know what we'll do!" Ida said. "We'll come back, and I'll bring the controller. Maybe that drone has some life left in it, and if I try to fly it, we'll see something move somewhere. It might just be wedged under something. Then we can run right in and grab it."

"Good idea," Ruth said. "Maybe later tonight when it's a little darker and Rupert can't see us so good. There's no fence around the perimeter, so we can run right in and grab it if we need to."

"We'll have to bring some dog treats to distract those dogs," Ida said. "They're biters."

Helen shot Ida a look. "Those sweet little things? I think they'd sooner cuddle you to death than bite you."

Ida held up her purse. "Really? Look what they did to my purse!"

"Never mind your purse," Nans said as they came to a stop next to Lexy's car. "Let's go over what we learned from Kingsley."

"Well, we learned that Olive and Rupert were pretty chummy with the sister. Maybe that's who Rupert's having the affair with," Ruth said.

"But we don't know that it's Rupert having the affair. It could be Olive," Helen pointed out.

"No, I don't think so. Kingsley didn't see any men coming over," Nans said.

"Maybe she was discreet about it," Ida suggested.

"We'll have to keep that as a possibility until we know more," Lexy said.

Helen's eyes flicked over toward the Jensens'. " Maybe Mrs. Jensen has more information."

Lexy thought she saw someone watching out one of the windows but couldn't be sure if it was just a reflection. "We definitely need to put her on our list of people to talk to."

"But not tonight," Nans said. "It's suppertime, and we don't want to disturb her. Plus I think our visit will be a lot better received if we bring some pastries from Lexy's bakery."

"Good idea!" Ida said. "We can pretend we're bringing sample pastries to all the neighbors on account of the Kingsleys' party. You know, Lexy could pretend she's trying to drum up more business."

"Hey, maybe she even really will get more business!" Ruth said.

"Maybe." Nans opened the passenger door of Lexy's car and flipped the seat up for Ruth, Ida, and Helen to contort themselves into the tiny back seat. "One other thing we found out from Kingsley is that Olive didn't need the money from her books. If what Kingsley said is true, they were living off of Olive's inheritance."

"Which gives Rupert an even bigger reason to pretend that she's alive. He wouldn't get any of that money if she were dead." Helen ducked her head, stuck her left leg into the car, and folded her body up as she slid into the back seat.

"And with the new book coming out, the royalties will go straight to their bank account." Ruth followed Helen into the back seat.

"But what about the sister?" Ida asked, pausing at the car door. "If they were close, the sister would notice Olive was missing."

"Not if the sister was in on it with him," Nans said.

"Good thinking," Ida said. "Which means tomorrow we need to take a trip out and talk to Olive's sister."

***

Lexy dropped the ladies off at the retirement center, where they rushed in and hurried to catch that night's bingo game. She had texted Jack about dinner earlier in the day, and they'd settled on Chinese food, which she picked up on the way home.

Jack pulled in just as she was wrestling the takeout bag out of the back seat of her car.

"I'll get that." He grabbed the handles of the bag and placed a kiss on the top of her head, sliding his free arm around her as they walked up to the front door. Sprinkles erupted in a chorus of barking as soon as Lexy slipped her key into the lock.

"Hey, girl." Lexy bent down to pet the dog as she wiggled and shimmied in front of them.

"I'll set out the plates. I'm starving." Jack headed toward the kitchen. Sprinkles, smelling the Chinese food, immediately abandoned Lexy to follow him.

Lexy wasn't far behind and pulled the cardboard containers out of the bag while Jack got plates out of the cabinets. Soon the aroma of sweet-and-sour chicken, beef teriyaki, and jumbo fried shrimp filled the small kitchen.

They loaded their plates and settled at the small kitchen table, with Sprinkles on the floor between them, eagerly looking up for a handout. Lexy cut off a little piece of broccoli that didn't have any sauce on it and handed it to the dog, who seemed oblivious that she was getting the least desirable piece of food.

"So what trouble did you guys get yourselves into today?" Jack asked over the piece of teriyaki.

"We didn't get into any trouble." Lexy poured some duck sauce on her rice. "Well, Nans and the ladies might have. They insisted on accompanying me to the consultation I had with Caspian Kingsley about the brunch I'm catering for him, and they almost fell into the Pendletons' pond."

"Uh huh." Jack dipped his teriyaki into the puddle of sauce on his plate. "What were they doing near the pond?"

"I'm pretty sure you could make a good guess."

"Looking for a body?"

"Spot on. But they didn't find one. It's too murky." Lexy chewed sweet-and-sour chicken thoughtfully then ventured a question to Jack. "Did you find out anything more?"

"No calls have come in, so as far as the police are concerned, there was no murder, but I did manage to take a little detour when I was out on a call, and I scoped out the backyard. I did see a big stain on the cement just like you said." Jack sighed. "Unfortunately, I can't get out there to test it to see if it's blood."

"But you do think it is," Lexy said eagerly.

"Of course. Based on what you told me. The trick is trying to prove it or find some kind of evidence that gives us probable cause to go in there."

"I found out a little bit of information on the Pendletons from Caspian Kingsley," Lexy said.

Jack's left brow quirked up. "Really? I'll tell you what I found out if you tell me what you found out."

"You found something out?" Lexy's heart warmed at the fact that Jack was investigating the case even though it wasn't official police business. Their relationship had really progressed. Once he would have scoffed at her. Now he took what she said more seriously and was helping out even though he could get in trouble at work.

Jack nodded. "You first though."

Lexy relayed the information Kingsley had told them about Olive's sister and the inheritance. She reiterated their suspicions that Rupert wanted Olive out of the way because he was having an affair, but he didn't want to lose out on her money, so he'd hidden the body somewhere.

"Since Olive is known to be reclusive at times, it's not hard for him to pretend she's just hiding away in her home office, writing," Lexy said.

"That's what I was thinking too. I did some more digging because I figured the motive probably has something to do with money. Olive did inherit a lot. Unfortunately, I can't look into their bank accounts or other finances without a warrant, which I won't be able to get. I was able to determine that their mortgage is current, and there's no foreclosure, but there were a couple of late payments and some dings in the collections database. Looks like they have...or *had* money trouble."

"But don't they have a lot of money if Olive inherited a bundle?"

"I'm not sure about that. But even a bundle can be spent pretty quickly."

"But if that money is gone, then why kill her?"

"Well, you did mention something about him having an affair, right? We both know that's the other reason most murders occur."

"Yeah, we were thinking maybe it's the sister, because they are close, and I think she would have said something by now if she'd lost contact with Olive." Something niggled at Lexy's brain. Something that Kingsley had said. "Kingsley said he saw another woman over there that he thought was either the maid or Olive's assistant."

"That's right," Jack said. "The little research I was able to do did come up with an assistant." Jack scrunched up his face and thought. "I think her name was Connie... yeah, that's right, Connie

Davis. I'm not sure about a maid. Doesn't seem like they could afford one."

"Connie Davis. Huh. Never heard of her." Lexy filed the name away for future use. She'd have Nans and the gang do some research on this Connie Davis. Maybe she was the one Rupert was having the affair with? If not, maybe she would know something about the affair or at least could be questioned about what was going on with Rupert and Olive. She could be a gold mine of information if she was Olive's assistant. They just had to approach her the right way.

Lexy reached across the table and put her hand on top of Jack's. "Thanks for having faith in me and helping us out. I know you're taking a risk at your job, so I really appreciate it."

"No problem, cupcake. I'm happy to help you, and besides, if there was a murder in town, I want to solve it even if there isn't any official evidence right now."

"Yeah, well, I just hope we *can* solve it."

"Don't worry. Either you, Nans, and the ladies will break the case, or some evidence will come to light. Something's bound to break soon, because you can't hide a body for very long. Sooner or later, they always turn up."

Eight

Even though Ruth drove a big blue Oldsmobile and the ladies were not without transportation, they'd talked Lexy into driving them over to Susan's house the next day. Lexy hadn't resisted much. She wanted to hear what the woman had to say herself, not to mention that she wasn't exactly sure that it was safe—or legal—for Ruth to drive. On the way over, she told them about Jack's visit to the house and how he'd noticed the stain on the patio, as well as the research he'd done on the Pendletons' finances and the identity of the assistant.

"I knew Jack wouldn't let us down," Nans said. "It's great that he's helping us out on the sly, but since he can't do anything officially, I think it's up to us to find the evidence to nail Rupert."

"And to find my drone," Ida chimed in from the back seat.

"I figured he wouldn't be able to look into their financials," Ruth said. "So last night I went to the community center to watch *Wheel of Fortune*. You know Mildred Dowse always watches it on the big screen in there on Fridays."

Nans swung around in her seat. "And Mildred still works at the bank!"

"Yes, she does, and when I happened to just casually mention the Pendletons, she told me that Rupert had come in every other Tuesday and gotten a whopper of a cashier's check." Ruth lowered her voice. "She's not supposed to tell anyone specifics about people's banking, but Mildred and I go way back."

"How much?" Nans asked.

"Ten thousand dollars!"

"Well, that certainly is interesting," Ida said. "I wonder what he would need that for. Maybe he's buying property or something."

"My bet is on the 'or something,'" Nans said.

"This case is shaping up! We have more research to do on Connie Davis and those mysterious cashier's checks," Helen said.

"Yeah, but maybe after we talk to Susan, we can head back over to the Pendletons'. I have the controller in my new purse," Ida persisted.

"Maybe, Ida, but the research is of the utmost importance. We have to get all the information and clues together before we make an incorrect assumption. Kingsley mentioned a maid, and we're not sure if the other woman he saw was this Connie person or a maid. Susan could be a totally innocent party, but I hope whatever she tells us today will shed some light on this situation," Nans said.

"That's the house, number seventeen." Ruth pushed her face into the front seat of Lexy's car as she pointed toward a small, blue, ranch-style home. Lexy pulled over to the curb. The neighborhood was modest, the houses probably built about twenty-five or thirty years ago. Well kept up but not rich by any means.

"You think that's Susan's house?" Nans frowned at her smartphone, where she'd used her GPS app to guide Lexy to the address they'd Googled earlier. "I guess it is. She sure doesn't live the high life like her sister."

"That's what Kingsley said." Ruth pulled the lever on the back seat and tried to push it up even while Nans was still sitting in it. "What are you waiting for? Let's go question her and see if we can trip her up."

Nans popped the door open then got out and pushed the seat up for Ruth. "Now Ruth, this isn't an interrogation. We have to speak to her gently."

"Maybe if we'd brought some pastries, it would've broken the ice," Ida suggested.

"You're just saying that because you wanted to eat some on the way over," Nans said.

"I still don't know what you're going to ask her, and the pastries are always a good excuse to start a conversation. No one ever turns away old ladies with pastries," Ida said.

"It's easy. I'm going to tell her that Helen here is doing a piece in the paper on what it's like to be the sister of a famous author."

Helen had been a journalist her entire life, and now that she was retired, she worked part time for the local paper. Her contacts at the paper came in handy, as did the excuse that she was working on an article. Anyone who got suspicious could check that she really worked there, but the paper would never verify exactly on what, and if anyone got too nosey or demanded to know when the article would be printed, Helen simply told them it had been cancelled.

"That sounds like it really would make a good article. Maybe I'll actually write that," Helen said as Nans knocked on the door.

They stood lined up on the stoop, waiting for Susan to answer. When no one came, Nans knocked again.

Ida shaded her eyes and looked through the window at the side of the door. "Darn it, just our luck. She must not be home."

"Where do you think she could be?" Ruth asked.

"Probably with Rupert now that Olive is out of the way." Ida wiggled her eyebrows mischievously. "All the better for snooping around."

Ida hopped off the steps and sidled past the bushes, pressing her face right up to the big picture window.

"What do you see?" Helen asked as she skirted the hedge, angling her body sideways to move in beside Ida.

"Nothing much. Looks like a regular living room to me."

"Maybe we can see more through one of the other rooms." Nans walked around the side of the house. "And the neighbors won't be able to see us snooping over here."

They followed Nans, peeking in the windows of a room which must've been the spare bedroom. A white quilt lay on the bed. The walls were cream colored, and a blue-and-white area rug covered honey-colored hardwood floors. A little white bureau sat against one wall, and on top of it were dozens of pictures of a little black dog.

"Oh, that must be her precious Peekapoo," Helen said. "Isn't that sweet. She has pictures of him."

"No pictures of the son, though," Nans observed.

"Kingsley said they were estranged, so maybe she doesn't keep pictures of him out. Too painful," Ruth said. "I wonder how long they've been on the outs."

They moved on to the next window. This one must've been the master bedroom, as it featured a queen-size bed with a colorful comforter. The room was neat as a pin. On the opposite wall was a low dresser with a TV on top. The closet door was slightly ajar, and some clothes were laid out at the foot of the bed. "She sure is different from the sister. Everything's in its place. 'Course, that makes sense if she was a librarian. That's what you found online, Ruth, right?" Helen asked.

"That's right. She's retired now, though. Looks like she has enough money to live comfortably but doesn't spend it frivolously like the Pendletons."

"I'm surprised with all that family money that she lives in this tiny little ranch," Ruth said as they went around the other side of the house and peeked in the doorway to the kitchen. Like the rest of the house, it was neatly apportioned. A modest kitchen table sat in the eat-in kitchen, sheer curtains on the windows. It was serviceable and clean but looked like it hadn't been updated in several years.

"Maybe she likes the security of having the money. Or maybe they didn't inherit as much as we're thinking," Nans said.

"Even if she did have a lot, that doesn't mean she wants to spend it all. Look at Myrna Hastings. She's a millionaire but lives like she's on Social Security," Ruth pointed out.

"Well, one thing's for sure: she doesn't have much to hide," Nans said as they came back around to the front. "There was nothing online that indicated anything out of the norm. She was married. Had a son. Worked in the library."

"Boring," Ida said.

"Hardly the type of person that would have an affair with her brother-in-law," Lexy added.

"Ha! Those are the type that usually do. All those repressed emotions or something." Ida peeked into the side door to the garage. "Her car's not here."

"Well, I wouldn't expect it to be if she didn't answer the door." Nans squinted toward the end of the driveway. "She must have been here at some point, because the mailbox flag is up."

"Oh, goody." Ida rubbed her hands together and rushed down to the mailbox. "Let's see what she's sending out. Maybe it's a love letter to Rupert."

Ida flipped the door open and reached her hand in then pulled it back out, a small square letter clutched between her fingers. The envelope was a thick cream-colored paper. The address on the front was neatly done in black pen

"It's addressed to Brent Chambers, 121 Forest Ave., Oakdale, Kentucky," Ida said.

"Brent? Why does that name sound familiar?" Ruth asked.

"I think that's the name of her son. Isn't that what Kingsley said?" Nans asked.

"Yes, it was. I remember distinctly," Lexy answered.

"So, it looks like she was sending a letter to the son." Helen's eyes got misty. "I hope she's trying to reconcile with him. I can't imagine what it would be like to be estranged from my son."

"Well, that's nice," Ida said. "But it doesn't help us with the investigation. And if we don't get a move on to get my drone back, *I'm* going to be the one that's estranged from my grandson."

"This might give us another lead," Nans said.

"But he lives all the way in Kentucky. And he hasn't been in touch with his mother. I doubt he knows anything that's going on." Ida looked disgusted.

A movement at the end of the street caught Lexy's eye, and she glanced down to see the mail truck. Nans must've seen it too, because she said in a hushed voice, "Put that back in the mailbox, Ida. The mailman is coming."

"Yeah, it's a federal offense to tamper with the mail," Helen said.

"I wasn't tampering. I was just looking." Ida held the letter out to the mailman. "Susan wanted to make sure this got mailed."

The mailman accepted it with a nod then passed a pile of mail to Ida, which she stuffed into the box as the others started back to the car.

"At least we know Susan was home earlier today. Otherwise her mailbox would've been full," Nans said.

"And we know she wants to reach out to the son," Ruth added.

"But the question is, does that have something to do with her sister's murder?" Helen asked.

"Time will tell." Nans turned to Ida. "For now, I say we take a drive over to the Pendleton place and see if we can dig up the drone. I don't think Rupert knows about it, so it's gotta still be out there in the yard with the incriminating video. If we can find the video, then we'll be home free."

"And if we can't?" Ruth asked.

"Then it looks like we have a lot more research to do."

Nine

The darkening sky dampened Lexy's spirits as she drove the short distance to the Pendleton house. Tomorrow was the Kingsleys' brunch, and she didn't want it to be cancelled because of bad weather.

"I hope we're not in for a rainy spell." She anxiously eyed the dark clouds moving in overhead.

Ruth whipped out her iPad. "The weather application says rain tonight, but tomorrow should be okay. We should be all set for the Kingsley event that we're catering."

Lexy narrowed her eyes at the rearview mirror. "*We?*"

"Why yes. It seemed to me that Caspian Kingsley was very much looking forward to us assisting you. Isn't that right, girls?"

"Yes. In fact, I would say we are probably what sold your services to him."

Lexy chuckled as she pulled up to the curb a few houses down from the Pendletons'. "Gee, really? And I thought I had secured the job over the phone all on my own days before. Well, good thing I have you guys by my side."

"Darn tootin'." Nans hopped out of the car, pulling the seat forward to let the other ladies out of the back.

Ida was already digging in her purse. She pulled out the controller and hurried up to the sidewalk, calling over her shoulder. "We're in luck. It looks like no one's home. We can do a thorough search. I just hope those attack dogs aren't out."

She stopped at the southeast corner of the property, pushing a few buttons on the controller. She pulled the joysticks this way and that, her eyes scanning the yard the whole time. "Do you ladies see any activity? It could be buried under something, maybe some old leaves. Do you see any moving?"

Lexy scanned along with them, but she didn't see any movement.

"Let's try over here." Nans walked over to the front facing the house. "We don't know where the dogs would've hidden it, but there's a stone bench over there and the remnants of what looks like a rock garden. Those seem like likely places, don't they, Lexy?"

"Sprinkles likes to hide her toys under things, and those would work," Lexy said.

They stayed on the sidewalk. The range of the controller was more than adequate from the sidewalk, so they didn't have to step onto the Pendleton property. But much as Ida tried, they did not see any sign of the drone.

"Maybe it's run out of batteries?" Ruth said.

"How much life did it have left in it?" Helen asked.

Ida pressed her lips together. "I don't know. Jason never said. 'Course, he didn't know I was gonna be flying it."

Ida cast about desperately, and Lexy could tell she was really getting worried about what might happen if she had to tell Jason she'd lost the drone. The neighbors on one side had a chain-link fence delineating their property from the Pendletons'. Old shrubs, a woodpile, and part of a stone wall ran next to it.

Lexy pointed to it. "This looks like a good place for the dogs to hide something."

Ida ran over, skulking along the edge of the fence, her fingers gripping the controllers, twisting this way and that, angling her head to see if there was any movement.

"If it's wedged between any of these rocks, though, it won't be able to move much," Helen said. "Maybe we should start looking under them."

Lexy glanced around at the yard and the house. She didn't see anyone moving around. If Rupert wasn't home, than what was the harm in looking under a few rocks? "Okay, but I think we better be quick. Rupert might come home, and besides I need to get to the bakery."

"I'll be quick." Nans bent down and started flipping over rocks. "We wouldn't want you to run short on pastries."

"Certainly not!" Ida said.

"Especially since you eat most of them," Helen added good-naturedly.

Lexy joined them, flipping over rocks and stones and looking under old rotted logs. But all they found were spiders and slugs. They were almost ready to give up when...

"*Woof!*"

"*Snarl!*"

"*Growl!*"

"It's the killer dogs!" Ida dropped the controller and held her hands up, palms out. The dogs stopped in front of them, barking and snapping.

Lexy had to admit they did look a little ferocious, but she doubted the tiny balls of fur would hurt them.

"They're probably just protecting their territory by instinct. I'm sure they're harmless." She bent down and held her hand out for them to sniff. "Here doggie, doggie."

They stopped their snarling and looked at Lexy curiously, tilting their heads from side to side. The black one ventured over, sniffing at her fingers. The apricot one followed, letting Lexy pat it behind the ears. She turned back to look up at the ladies, who were standing with their backs against the fence. "See? They're harmless."

"What are you doing trespassing in my yard?!"

Lexy jerked her head back around to see Rupert storming out from the back of the house.

"Dang. I don't think he's as harmless as his dogs," Ruth said.

Rupert stormed up to them, his face contorted in anger.

"Heya!" He snapped his fingers, and the dogs reluctantly turned from Lexy and ran to his side. "Aren't you the same busybodies that were here the other day?"

Nans straightened indignantly. "We're not busybodies. We are fans."

Rupert's eyes snapped to Ida, who was bending down to pick up her controller. "What's that thing she's got? Isn't she the senile one?"

"That's right." Nans leaned forward and whispered, "I wouldn't rile her up. Don't ask what that thing is that she has. You'll be sorry."

Rupert frowned at Ida then glanced uncertainly back at the house. "Well, you ladies are trespassing. I told you before, we don't like fans to just show up. Do I have to call the police?"

"No. No police. We just saw your dogs, and since we are dog lovers, we wanted to come over and pet them," Lexy said.

"Oh, come on, Lexy, tell the truth," Ruth said. The rest of them shot her quizzical looks.

"You know as well as I do," Ruth continued, "that we were here to get a glimpse of Olive Pendleton."

"Oh, *right*," Nans said, following Ruth's lead. "That's right. You're her husband, right? Is she inside?" Nans made a point of trying to look around Rupert's shoulder.

Rupert eyed them suspiciously. "No. She's not inside."

"Well, it is kind of funny that she's never around when we come here," Helen said. "Almost as if you are hiding something."

"Not that it's any of your business, but my wife is in Europe." Rupert pulled his phone out of his back pocket, thumbed through a few screens, then turned it toward them. "See? She took this picture just yesterday. You can see her standing there plain as day with her sister, holding up the Paris paper with her picture on it. She has a new book release next week, and her books are very popular in France, so they did a little article and featured her in the paper."

They all craned their necks toward the phone. Lexy's brows pinched together in puzzlement as she stared at the picture. It was Olive Pendleton, with another woman who looked a lot like her, holding up a paper. They were the same height and had the same hair color and style, but their facial features were different. Where one had delicate features, the other was chiseled in stone. Sisters. The Eiffel Tower loomed in the background.

Lexy's heart tumbled when she saw the date on the paper. It was yesterday's date. If what she was seeing was correct, Olive Pendleton was in France and very much alive.

Ten

"Those photos could be photoshopped," Ruth said later that day as they sat around Nans' dining room table.

"I know photos can be photoshopped, but do you really think *those* were?" Nans picked a brownie off the crystal platter in the center of the table. "Rupert doesn't seem savvy enough."

"How would he even do that?" Helen asked. "They looked like genuine pictures of France, and there was the newspaper...oh, but if he was in on it with the sister, maybe she took the picture and photoshopped Olive into it."

"But the sister isn't in Europe, because she put that letter in her mailbox," Ida pointed out.

"Hmm..." Nans pressed her lips together then snapped her fingers. "Wait! Today is Monday. Susan could have put that letter in on Saturday. The mailman doesn't come on weekends anymore."

"Plenty of time for her to take an overnight flight to Europe and be in Paris in time to get the paper," Lexy said.

"Right." Nans turned to Ruth. "Ruth, you know the most about this sort of thing. Did it look altered to you?"

"I didn't get close enough to say for sure, unfortunately." Ruth picked a lemon square off the tray. "But if I had to guess, I'd say it was altered."

"It had to have been. Olive couldn't possibly be in France. We saw her die," Lexy said.

Ida picked up a sugar cube with the bird-claw tongs, hovered over her coffee, and then dropped it in with a splash. "Maybe that wasn't Olive."

Lexy glanced at the whiteboard. "But you have all that evidence. It all points to Olive being killed."

"Only because that was the original assumption. We made the evidence to prove that Rupert would want to kill Olive, but maybe we were wrong all along," Nans said.

"No. No." Ruth shook her head. "That picture is all part of Rupert's plan. He wants the world to think Olive is still alive, and what better way than to have an actual picture of her? And her being in France would explain why she doesn't show up for the book signing scheduled next week for her new book."

"Good point. That *would* be a clever plan," Lexy said.

"At any rate, someone is still dead, and my bet is that Rupert killed them." Nans stood in front of the whiteboard. "Let's discuss our new clues."

"Something really bothers me. Those cash deposits—they might indicate a different motive for the murder," Ruth said.

"You mean blackmail?" Ida asked.

"Yes. What if Olive was blackmailing someone, and *that's* why she was killed?" Ruth suggested.

"But Rupert killed Olive. She wouldn't be blackmailing him, would she?" Helen asked.

Ruth shrugged. "Maybe. Maybe not. But how do we know for sure that Rupert is the killer?"

Lexy leaned back in her chair. Ruth had a point. They'd *assumed* Rupert was the killer because Rupert and Olive lived in the house. Could the killer be someone else?

"If it's not Rupert, then why would he photoshop the pictures to pretend Olive was alive?" Ida asked.

Ruth pressed her lips together and nodded at Ida. "Good point. Maybe they aren't photoshopped."

Helen threw her hands up in the air. "So, where does that leave us then?"

"A big fat nowhere," Nans said. "The only thing we're sure of is that someone died and someone else is hiding the body."

Ruth got up and paced the room. "Okay, let's see what we have so far. Someone was killed by someone else inside the Pendleton home. So that means the killer is either one of the Pendletons or someone who has access to the house."

"The sister had access to the house," Ida said.

"And the assistant. Kingsley said he saw her there quite often," Lexy said.

"He said he saw another woman. He thought it might be her assistant or a maid," Ruth said.

"It makes sense an assistant would be there. Probably went there every day or on most days. Connie Davis. Google her, Ruth, and see what you can find," Nans said.

"I'm on it," Ruth replied.

"Now the other things we have." Nans took over for Ruth, pacing the room. "Those mysterious cashier's checks. That could indicate blackmail. Or perhaps they were buying property or making a big purchase."

Ruth looked up from her iPad. "I didn't find any record of them buying property."

"It's too bad there's no way for us to tap into their bank accounts and see how they are moving money around." Nans glanced at Ruth out of the corner of her eye. "Is there, Ruth?"

"Not legally..."

"Illegally?"

"I might know someone," Ruth said. "But I think we should track down the other clues first before we stoop to that."

"Right. Jack might not like that." Nans shot Lexy a look, and she nodded.

"Whatever it is, I'm pretty sure the sister must be mixed up in it," Helen said. "Because either she is in on photoshopping the pictures, or she's in Europe with Olive. And we know Olive was home the day of the murder because Rupert said she was at the house napping. He didn't say she was in Europe. Unless, of course, he was lying then, too."

"Well, at least this part is the truth." Ruth tapped the screen of her iPad. "There really was an article about Olive in the Paris paper yesterday. But I can't find any record of her flying out there. My friend Janet gave me travel agent access, and I didn't see her in the database."

"Could she be flying under another name?" Nans asked. "I know celebrities sometimes use a different name in the public database to keep the paparazzi at bay. Their real name is listed official-ly, of course, but that's only on the internal records. Some of them even have people stand in for them at minor social events."

"I hardly think Olive Pendleton rates as a celebrity," Helen said.

"You'd be surprised." Nans shrugged. "Novelists can be very popular."

"If Olive wasn't the one on that plane, then that only supports my theory of the pictures being photoshopped," Ruth said.

"Which means the sister *is* in on it," Helen added.

"Which supports my theory of an affair," Ida said.

"Looks like we only know one thing for sure. Someone was murdered. It could be love or money. An affair or blackmail," Nans said. "Either way, it looks like Rupert Pendleton is hiding something."

Eleven

The next morning, Lexy was glad to take a break from investigating and focus on affairs at her bakery. Her assistant and best friend since high school, Cassie, was helping her finalize the menu for the Kingsley brunch the next day. They didn't have a lot of customer action, so they hung out in the kitchen, mixing and baking their usual cookies, cupcakes, bars, and pies while discussing the Kingsleys' menu and taking turns running out front to service the customers that came in.

"I already have several different quiches planned," Lexy said as she poured a tablespoon of vanilla extract into the batch of sugar cookies she was mixing. "But I think we should make up some finger sandwiches, too. I have a great cranberry chicken salad recipe."

"That sounds delish." Cassie was bent over at the waist, her eyes level with the table, her pink-tipped, spiked blonde hair bobbing up and down like a bird's crest as she applied turquoise fondant hearts to the side of a cake. Lexy had hired Cassie when she'd first opened the bakery because she knew she could trust her. Since then, Cassie had become quite adept at cake decorating and was proving to be an excellent baker herself.

"So, what is going on with the Pendleton case?" Cassie asked. Lexy had told Cassie all about the murder they'd witnessed with Ida's drone and had been keeping her up to date with the subsequent events. In return, Cassie, who was married to Jack's partner John Darling, promised to pass along anything she heard from John.

"Oh! Did I forget to tell you? Yesterday, Rupert showed us pictures on his iPhone of Olive in France!"

Cassie's head jerked up from her task. "You mean she's not dead?"

"No, we still think she's dead. Ruth said that he could have photoshopped them to make it look like she is alive and in Europe."

"That's true. My brother does a lot with Photoshop, and he makes all kinds of crazy memes and other weird photos." Cassie bent back down to her task. "So you think the husband did that to perpetuate this plan of pretending she's still alive. What do you think he's done with the body, though? John said it's pretty hard to hide a body for any length of time."

"That's what Jack said, too. We're not sure, but we think maybe she's in the pond."

"But what do you think his plan is? I mean, he can't pretend she's in Europe forever. Doesn't she have a book signing next week?" Cassie straightened back up and tapped her finger on her lips. "And I think I read something about an author conference too."

"We think he might be planning to pretend that she disappears." Lexy plopped the dough out onto a floured marble slab, grabbed her rolling pin, and started rolling it out. "You know, like what happened with Agatha Christie back in the forties."

"That's right. Her car was found mysteriously abandoned. I bet that would generate a lot of interest for Olive's books. Probably more interest than if she just died." Cassie opened the oven, grabbed some oven mitts, and pulled out a tray of brownies, allowing the smell of chocolate to perfume the room. "But why pretend she's in Europe? That doesn't seem to make much sense."

Lexy rolled the dough to the perfect thickness. "Not much of what he's doing is making sense. Maybe he wants to pretend she disappeared over in Europe because then the police here won't get involved?" Lexy picked up a heart-shaped cookie cutter and started cutting out the cookies, pressing down into the dough and then prying up the shapes and transferring them to a silicone baking sheet.

"Good point. Maybe he's not so stupid after all," Cassie said.

The bells on the front door jangled, indicating a customer.

"My turn." Lexy peeled off her food-service gloves, tossed them in the trash, and headed out front, where four gray-haired ladies stood in front of the pastry case with their heads bent together.

There was something familiar about the ladies, and Lexy figured it was that they reminded her of Nans, Ruth, Ida, and Helen, who often came into the bakery to relieve her of the brownie ends and broken cookies.

"I think we should get cookies this time, Florence." A lady in a navy-blue shirt tapped the glass case in front of Lexy's display of frosted cookies. Since it was summertime, she'd done a variety of different flowers in all colors.

"They look spectacular if you present them in a basket," Lexy said.

"I don't know," a woman in yellow said. "We had cookies last time. I think we should go for bars and brownies this time."

"You could do both," Lexy suggested.

"True." Navy-Blue Shirt looked up at Lexy. "Do you have a discount for the ladies' auxiliary?"

"Ladies' auxiliary?"

"Yes, we put on functions every month." Yellow Shirt narrowed her eyes. "You didn't know?"

"Oh, yes! Sorry. I've heard about your functions from my grandmother," Lexy lied. Best to butter up the customers and make them feel important.

"We're trying to get Olive Pendleton to speak at our next one. She's coming out with a new book, you know," Navy-Blue Shirt said.

A third woman, this one in a red shirt, huffed, "Except she hasn't replied to us."

"I'm sure she's very busy," Yellow Shirt said.

"I heard she was in France," Lexy said.

The ladies frowned at her in unison, their faces folding into dozens of wrinkles. "France? We doubt that."

"Why?" Lexy asked.

"We are her official Brook Ridge Falls fan club. And we know all of her comings and goings. We weren't alerted to any trip to France," Red Shirt said.

"And furthermore, I don't think she's left her house," Navy Shirt added.

"How would you know that?" Lexy asked.

The ladies exchanged guilty looks. "Well...we sort of keep an eye on her."

Now Lexy remembered why they looked familiar. These were the people she'd seen driving by in the car in the Pendletons' neighborhood. If they kept an eye on the house, they might have seen something. She needed to butter them up, loosen their tongues, and keep them talking.

"We're not stalkers," Red Shirt added.

"Of course not! This is your first time buying cookies in here, isn't it?" Lexy asked.

The ladies nodded in unison.

"Well then, this order is on me. Pick out whatever you want, and I'll fill up a box for you. In fact, why don't you try some samples." Lexy pulled out the tray of bite-sized samples she kept and handed it over the case. The ladies passed them around, carefully choosing their little pieces and making num-num noises as they sampled.

Lexy took the opportunity to interrogate them. "I'm catering a brunch right near the Pendletons'. Olive sure is eccentric."

"I'll say," Navy-Blue Shirt said. "Why, do you know she sometimes has her assistant go to author conferences in her stead?"

"You don't say," Lexy said. "Do they look alike?"

Yellow Shirt shrugged and swallowed a big chunk of frosted brownie. "They're the same height, same hair, which I think is done on purpose, and if the assistant doesn't talk to anyone that personally knows Olive, then all the papers see is someone that looks like Olive doing things Olive should be doing."

"But why does she do that?" Lexy asked. "I would think she would want to go to those places herself."

"No. In fact, if you go to our official fan page on Facebook, you'll see that she is somewhat reclusive."

"Then you think she wouldn't want to travel off to France." Lexy accepted the tray back from the ladies, put it in the case, and started constructing the white bakery box. "Pick out whatever you want, and I'll fill the box for you."

"Yeah, that's why we don't think she's in France." Navy Shirt tapped her fingers over some coconut-covered brownies then moved to some macaroons. Lexy dutifully put two of each in the box.

"Because she likes to stay home?" Lexy asked.

"Well, that and the fact that she hasn't left her house all week." Yellow Shirt bent and squinted into the case. "Can we have some of these chocolate scones?"

"Sure." Lexy picked up chocolate scones and nestled them in bakery paper then laid them in the box. "But how do you know she hasn't left her house all week?"

"Like we said, we're on watch. We monitor her comings and goings. Sometimes we even get a photograph for the page. There's a few others who take shifts for us. Between us, we've been there quite a bit this week, and the only activity we've seen has been the sister coming and going in her little white Fiat. In fact, seems she's still there. Oh! And the husband took his truck out last Saturday and came back with a load of stuff for that gazebo they're building. He was gone an awfully long time. But Olive hasn't left that house all week."

As the ladies picked out pastries, Lexy put them into the box on autopilot, her mind whirling with new information. Was it possible they had been watching the house the entire week? Surely they wouldn't be able to watch it all day and night, but if Olive had left to fly to Europe, wouldn't they have seen her? And why was the sister still there when she lived just on the other side of town?

Too bad they hadn't been there when Olive fell off the balcony. They'd have witnessed it and called the cops. But in order to have seen Olive fall, they would have to have been in the backyard or in the Kingsleys' backyard. The patio wasn't visible from anywhere else.

"Couldn't Olive have taken the Fiat? Borrowed it or something?"

"Oh no, she only *ever* drives the red Cadillac."

The ladies left, thanking Lexy profusely, with their overstuffed box. Lexy couldn't wait to tell Nans and the ladies this latest discovery, because everything the four women had said further reinforced the theory that Olive was dead and Rupert and the sister had had something to do with it.

Twelve

"Now why didn't I think of that?" Ruth tapped furiously on the iPad. "I should've known to look for Olive's fan club page."

"Well, you can't think of everything." Nans pretended she was studying her nails. "That's my job."

"Yep, here it is." Ruth slid the iPad around. The page banner showed a sampling of Olive's books along with a picture of her. The posts were filled with sightings of Olive and some selfies from the four ladies who had been in Lexy's bakery.

"Look! This is her assistant." Helen pinched her fingers together over one of the photographs and pulled them apart to enlarge it. The photograph was of a woman with blond hair like Olive, large sunglasses, and a scarf wrapped around her blond hair, obscuring part of her face.

"She does look like Olive," Ruth said.

"But it says below this is Connie," Lexy said. "The ladies at the bakery said she has Connie stand in for her sometimes when she doesn't want to go to events."

Nans' brows mashed together. "Really? You don't think that could be Connie in the Paris picture, do you?"

Ruth shook her head. "No. Look. Here is a picture of Olive with Connie. They don't look that much alike when looking at their faces straight on. It's only at a distance with the scarf obscuring her face."

Lexy studied the picture. Sure enough, the two women were similar, but the picture of Olive that Rupert had on his phone definitely was not Connie.

"Well, this is confusing," Ida said. "Is Olive in France or is Connie in France?"

"It could be that no one is in France," Ruth said. "Look, to show you how easy it is to photoshop, I have taken the liberty of sending Mona to China."

Ruth tapped on the iPad and brought up a picture of Nans standing on top of the Great Wall of China. It looked pretty good, but on close inspection, Lexy could tell it was faked.

"This is okay, Ruth, but anyone who gives it a good gander can tell that you messed with it," Ida said.

"Well, sure they can." Ruth took the iPad back and scowled at Ida. "This was just a quick thing I did up, and besides, we didn't get a good gander at Rupert's. For all we know, it was just as unprofessional. I merely wanted to illustrate what is possible."

"Okay. So this doesn't get us any further than we were yesterday except now we know a little bit more about Olive's assistant." Nans got a whiteboard marker, went to the whiteboard, jotted something down, and then turned to Ruth. "Did you do any research on her?"

Ruth looked pleased. "As a matter of fact, I did. Connie has been Olive's assistant for quite a few years now. They work together closely, and she lives here in town. If Olive met with foul play, I think it would be only a matter of time before Connie realized something was amiss."

"Unless Connie is in on it," Ida suggested.

"Right. So far we've just been going on the assumption that it's Rupert and the sister. Maybe it's Rupert and Connie," Nans said.

"Or Connie and the sister," Helen added.

"The ladies that came to the bakery did say that they'd only seen the sister leave the house. I guess she drives a little white Fiat," Lexy said. "Oh, and Rupert went out and got some building stuff for the gazebo. But not Olive. They haven't seen her all week."

"Well, that's new information," Nans said.

"And they seem to think the Fiat has been at the house all week," Lexy said.

"Meaning that Susan has been there since Olive was murdered," Ida said.

"Right."

"With Olive out of the picture, Rupert and Susan are free to do as they please," Helen said.

"But there is one thing that bothers me still." Nans stood at the whiteboard, studying the clues. "If Rupert and Susan killed Olive because they were having an affair, then what is the deal with the cashier's checks? Something else is going on here."

"The plot thickens," Ruth said. "A simple affair might not be the only motive. Or maybe it has nothing to do with the affair and everything to do with money."

A doorbell chimed inside Ida's purse, and all heads swiveled toward it.

"Must be my phone." Ida rummaged in the purse and pulled out an iPhone, her face collapsing into a frown. She looked up at them with serious eyes. "It's Jason. He needs the drone for Tuesday. Ladies, we have a priority-one mission."

Thirteen

Lexy couldn't believe Nans and the ladies had talked her into driving them back to Castle Heights. The big catering job at the Kingsleys' was tomorrow, and she still had a lot of prep to do, but when Ruth threatened to drive in her giant blue Oldsmobile, Lexy capitulated. Ruth was known to run over every curb and shrub in sight, and her driving had been getting worse. Lexy didn't want an accident and potential bodily injury of Nans or one of her friends on her conscience.

So later that day, she found herself parking her car a few houses down from the Pendletons'.

Ida clutched the controller in her hand and flipped it on. "I just hope we can find it. You know, Jason is a pretty big real estate agent. He has a million-dollar property that he needs the drone to take pictures of. I don't know what will happen if I don't produce the darn thing by Tuesday."

"Do you see any activity over there?" Ruth leaned against the car, her eyes looking in the direction of the Pendletons'.

"No, but the last time we didn't see anything, and we almost got eaten by those dogs," Ida said. "I say we stick to the neighbors' yards. This house here looks like the people are on vacation."

Ida trotted across the street and through someone's front yard, holding the remote in front of her and fiddling with the controls.

"Ida! Where are you going?" Ruth asked.

"We already tried this yesterday," Helen said.

"I'm just going to go down by the gazebo," Ida yelled from across the yard. "We didn't try near there."

The others looked at each other and shrugged then started across the front yard in her wake.

"Hey, what are you pretty ladies doing here?"

They jerked around in the direction of the voice to see a man sitting on his screened-in porch. He was wearing a white cotton T-shirt and two days' growth of beard and had a pyramid of beer cans stacked in front of him.

"Sorry, sir. We're just cutting through," Nans said.

"Why don't you come up and have a beer? Especially the pretty little one in the flowered shirt." The man gestured his beer can toward Helen, who blushed. Lexy had no idea why, but the guys always seemed to go for Helen. She hoped Helen would use the man's invitation to their advantage.

Helen sidled closer to the porch and smiled in at the man. "Well, I can't say as we have time. I'm Helen. What's your name?"

"Bud." The man took a sip from the beer. "Mighty hot out. Sure you don't want a beer? It'll cool you off. Always does. The missus is on vacation up to her sister's in Maine." He favored Helen with an exaggerated wink.

Lexy noticed that the man had a perfect view into the Pendletons' backyard from his perch on the porch. Was it possible he'd seen something?

"This is a great porch. I bet you take advantage of it a lot," Lexy said.

The man nodded. "Ayup. Sit out here most evenings. Most afternoons, too."

"You're nice and tucked away in there. I bet you see a lot of things from the neighbors here that they don't know you're seeing." Helen indicated the two neighboring backyards, one of which was the Pendletons'.

"I sure do. In fact, I saw you ladies over there at the Pendletons' the other day. What's it you're looking for, anyway?" The man pointed toward Ida, who was down at the edge of the property, pointing her controller toward the gazebo and apparently having no luck.

"A drone," Ruth said. At the man's confused look, she added, "Like a remote-control plane. You wouldn't happen to have seen one of those flying around or the dogs carrying one, would you?"

The man pressed his lips together then shook his head. "Nope, can't say as I saw that. Those three dogs sure do make a ruckus. Especially when the sister comes over with hers."

"And she comes over often, doesn't she?" Helen shot him her brightest smile, and Lexy figured she was buttering him up for more questions.

"Yep. They're as close as ducks in a pond."

"Must be kind of annoying for Rupert to have his sister-in-law over all the time. Do you know him well?" Nans asked.

"Nah. Not too much. Been to a few parties over there, but Rupert, well, he's a little henpecked. I don't think he'd say boo about having the sister over there. Especially not when she distracts Olive and leaves Rupert to ogle that cute maid they have running around."

"Maid?" Lexy asked.

"Oh yeah. They got one of those services. You know, the one with the green truck that comes around and cleans your house every so often.

We'd get one here, but the missus likes to do her own cleaning."

"And you think Rupert fancies this maid?" Nans asked.

Bud snorted. "Well, who wouldn't fancy her? She's young, blonde, and..." he let go of his beer long enough for his hands to form an hourglass shape.

"Do you think he has something going on with her?" Helen asked.

The man's eyes narrowed. "Now I didn't say that. I don't really know if Rupert is the type. But if he was and she was willing, I wouldn't blame him."

Ida came back with a look of disappointment marring her features. "I didn't get nothing down there... Oh, hello. Who are you?"

"I'm Bud. You want a beer? I was hoping your friend here would come up, but you'll do."

Ida scowled at him. "I don't think so, mister. I don't play second fiddle to no one."

"Ida!" Nans looked at her sharply. "Bud was just telling us about the Pendletons'. Now let's be cordial to him."

"Oh." Ida flashed him a smile. "Did you happen to see my drone flying around in their backyard the other day?"

"Nope, can't say as I did."

"And have you noticed anything strange over there?" Ruth asked.

"Not any stranger than usual. Though I have to say that gazebo they're building is kind of unusual. Looks like he's doing it piecemeal. Not a professional job. But then, that's Rupert. I'm surprised Olive's putting up with it."

Ida snorted. "She might not know what's going on."

"Why don't they just hire someone?" Lexy asked.

Bud frowned. "I'm not sure. I heard they had money troubles. But you never know with them. They throw big parties, but look at the place. It's a mess. You ask me, Rupert's a little off his rocker."

"Is Rupert home?" Nans asked.

"No. Saw him go out with the four dogs in the truck. Probably picking up Olive."

"Oh, Olive isn't home either?"

Bud shook his head. "Ain't seen her for a few days. Heard she was in Europe."

"Okay, well, nice meeting you, Bud." Nans grabbed Ruth and Ida's elbows and pulled them away from the house.

"Hey, I didn't get a chance to look for the drone over there. It could be over in the back, and I've got to find it, or I'm going to be in big trouble with Jason," Ida grumbled.

"Oh, Ida, stop your bellyaching. If worse comes to worst, you can just buy him a replacement. They sell them right on Amazon, you know," Nans said.

"They do?"

"'Course. They sell everything over there."

Nans swiveled her head back and forth as if making sure no one was watching as she speed walked toward the Pendletons' garage.

"Looks like the fan club doesn't watch the house all the time," Ruth said, glancing around. "They're not here now."

"Right. They couldn't possibly have twenty-four-hour surveillance, so we can't rely on their information," Nans said. "Which is why I'm going over now to take a little peek into the garage."

Nans pulled them down the driveway, sticking to the edge, where they would be hidden by the tall lilac bushes. When they reached the end, she sidled over in front of the doors, stood on her tip-toes, and looked in. She fell back on her heels and turned to them. "Well looks like the ladies might've been right. That white Fiat is sitting right in the garage. Susan might even be in the house right now."

"Just as we thought," Ida said.

"But another thing." Nans' brows knitted together. "The red Cadillac is not in there."

"Well, go figure that." Ida jumped up to get enough height to look in the window. "Oh yeah. It's not there. Did those fan club ladies tell you Olive only drove that car, Lexy?"

"They did."

"That fits perfectly with our disappearance theory," Ruth said. "Apparently it's well known that Olive drives that Cadillac. Rupert probably took it to some remote spot to be discovered later by the police when he reports Olive is missing. Just like Agatha Christie."

"And since Olive is dead, she can't really complain that someone else drove her car," Helen added.

Nans nodded. "That's right. And if I recall the Agatha Christie case, her car was found abandoned, and they never did find her until eleven days later."

"That's right," Helen said. "Hey, did either of you see the baseball bat in there?"

"The murder weapon?" Nans stood on her tiptoes and looked in again. "No. But I don't think that will help us. Without a body, the murder weapon is pretty much meaningless."

"I suppose you're right," Helen said. "Might come in handy once we find the body, though."

"*If* we find the body. If Rupert is trying to make like she disappeared, we may never find it."

Nans turned and started toward Lexy's car, keeping to the security of the lilacs but walking faster this time. "I'm sure that's what Rupert has planned, but we are going to foil his plans by finding it."

"Or the drone with the video on it," Ida said hopefully.

"Either one will prove she was murdered," Ruth said. "Doesn't matter."

"It matters to me," Ida argued.

Nans waved a hand to shush them. "Quiet now. Let me think. We need to find this maid. Ruth, can you Google the maid service with the green truck?"

"I think that's Happy Home Cleaners," Helen said.

"Good. Then let's find out who they have that cleans at the Pendletons'." Nans opened Lexy's car door and pushed the seat up, gesturing for the others to get in. "Hurry now, ladies. We need to get back to my place so we can figure out who this maid is and where she lives as well as find out more about Connie. We need to pay them both a visit. Maybe first thing tomorrow morning, we can..." Nans' voice trailed off, and she looked at Lexy. "Oh, shoot. We have the Kingsleys' brunch tomorrow morning."

Lexy had been hoping Nans and the ladies would've forgotten about that, but since they hadn't, and they seemed to have other things on their minds, Lexy saw the perfect way to give them an easy out and prevent them from tagging along to the brunch. "Oh, that's no problem. You guys don't have to help. Cassie is going to be there, and we can handle it. It's more important that you do your research."

"Oh, we wouldn't dream of leaving you in the lurch, would we, girls?" Nans asked.

"Of course not," the others agreed.

"Especially since it will give me an added chance to look for the drone," Ida said.

"That's right. We're a team," Ruth said. "We'll be waiting for you at the door to the retirement center first thing tomorrow morning!"

Fourteen

After Lexy dropped Nans and the ladies off, she rushed back to the bakery to finalize the plans for the Kingsley brunch with Cassie. Unlike the other events they'd catered, this one included food that needed to be kept hot, and she also needed refrigeration plus platters and display trays. Since she didn't have any of that type of equipment, she'd hired a company to provide it, and she wanted to double- and triple-check the scheduling to make sure things ran smoothly.

They spent the afternoon and well into the evening working out exactly how they would set it up. Then Lexy double-checked with the party supply company to make sure the tent would be set up early that morning and the appropriate chairs and tables would be provided. Lexy had hired a temporary chef to serve eggs and sausages and make toast out of her homemade bread, and she checked in with him as well.

When she was satisfied everything was perfect, she returned home, exhausted, with a box of éclairs she'd snagged from the bakery case. Jack was already home and had put a chicken in the oven, so Lexy didn't have to eat éclairs for supper. She'd definitely have them for dessert, though.

"I cooked, so you have to do the dishes," Jack said as they sat at the table, their stomachs full and their plates empty.

"Dessert first." Lexy pulled the éclairs out of the box and put them on a plate. She cut one in half and transferred it to her plate. She'd probably eat the other half, but for now it felt like she was being good and only eating half the dessert.

"Anything new on the Pendleton case?" she asked.

Jack shook his head. "Nothing. How about you?"

Lexy filled him in on what they had found out so far, including the visit to her bakery from the fan club.

"So you still think an affair is at the bottom of this?" Jack asked when she was done.

"Yes. And probably something financial too. Something's just not right about what's going on over there." Lexy bit into the éclair, the creamy custard exploding in her mouth, the sweetness tempered by the dark chocolate. They ate in silence, with the scratching of Sprinkles' nails on the floor as she pranced between them, hoping for a smidgen of the treat as accompaniment. But Lexy wouldn't give her a piece of the éclair. Chocolate was lethal to dogs, so Sprinkles would have to settle for one of her dental treats instead.

Jacked polished off the last bite and pushed his plate toward Lexy. "I wish there was more I could do to investigate. I know some real evidence has to turn up soon, but until then..." Jack shrugged.

"There might be something you can look into," Lexy said.

"What's that?"

"The ladies in Olive's fan club said that she always drove a red Cadillac. But when we were at her house yesterday, that car wasn't in the garage. The ladies said they hadn't seen it leave the house though."

"How would they know? Do they live in the neighborhood?"

"I don't think so. They said they kept a watch on the house."

"Oh, stalker fans."

Lexy laughed. "Sort of. These are just old ladies that have nothing better to do. I think they're harmless."

"Right. Just like Nans, Ruth, Ida, and Helen. They are old ladies with nothing to do...except they're far from harmless."

"Good point." Lexy cleared the dishes from the table and took them to the sink to wash. "Anyway, one of our working theories is that Rupert is planning on capitalizing on Olive's new release by pretending she's disappeared mysteriously. You know, like Agatha Christie did back in the twenties?"

Lexy glanced over her shoulder to see if Jack was following. He nodded.

"So he might have already driven the car to some remote place. Most likely in the middle of the night when the fan club ladies would be at home, tucked in their beds and not watching the house," Lexy continued.

"In which case he would've needed an accomplice to drive him back," Jack added.

"Good point. We didn't even think of that, but it further bolsters the theory of an affair."

"Sure does. Well, we can be on the lookout for a red Cadillac. It should stand out. I'll tell John and the patrol officers to keep an eye out. Maybe even take a ride down some of the less-traveled roads to see if we can find it," Jack said.

"Great. That would be awesome. If you could find it, it would really throw a wrench in Rupert's plans." Lexy flipped open the dishwasher and started loading. "If only we could somehow get into that pond. I'm sure he put Olive's body in there. And I think I know how he's keeping that body from floating up."

"And how is that?"

"They're building that gazebo, and he's doing it in a really odd manner. Normally you'd pour the foundation first, but for some reason they started on the walls, and now he's got bags of concrete sitting up there. I think it's misdirection. He wants it to *look* like he's using the concrete for the foundation, but what if he really used it to weigh Olive's body down? You know, by giving her cement shoes or something."

"I don't think cement shoes actually work. The body would decompose, and the skeleton would slip out of the cement. But I suppose he could weigh it down another way like wrapping her in a tarp or something and then weighing the sides of that down. It would take forever for that to decompose, and her body would be trapped inside it. She could be down there for a long time."

"A tarp..." Lexy closed her eyes, trying to remember what she'd seen on the viewscreen of the drone's controller. Had there been a tarp in the area, and was it now missing? She squeezed her eyes tight, trying to put herself in a mini hypnotic trance just like Helen had taught her. If she could get herself into that state, she'd be able to remember exactly what she'd seen. In her mind's eye, she pictured the drone zipping over the Kingsleys' yard then turning to look at the pond, the yard, and then the gazebo. "There was a blue tarp!"

"At the Pendletons'?" Jack asked.

"Yes. I distinctly remember it was near the gazebo. Of course, it didn't seem out of place because there was lumber underneath it."

"But when did you see it? Before or after Olive was killed?"

"Before. We saw it on the screen of the drone."

"And is it still there?"

"That I'm not sure of. But you can bet I'll be looking to see if it is when I cater the Kingsleys' brunch tomorrow morning."

Fifteen

The next day, Lexy was blessed with blue skies and moderate temperatures. Though it was summertime in New Hampshire and the day would probably get up into the mid-eighties, the morning for the brunch would be pleasant and in the upper seventies. A perfect day for her new venture.

She got to the Kingsleys' early, having picked up Nans, Ruth, Ida, and Helen, who were all dressed in crisp white aprons and carrying chef hats. At least they were taking the catering part of their mission seriously, even though Ruth had also been carrying her wetsuit, which they stored in the trunk. Lexy hoped Ruth wouldn't have an inclination to put it on.

Cassie had gotten there before her and was pulling the food out of the van. Lexy left the ladies unsupervised. She was worried about the kind of trouble they could get into on their own, but her first priority was making sure the brunch went off without a hitch. She busied herself checking the tent, making sure the tables were set up where she wanted them, and helping Cassie spread the white linen tablecloths on the tables. She double-checked the food stations, making sure everything was serviceable and looked fantastic.

They'd ordered little bouquets of daisies in crystal vases that they put on each of the tables where the guests would sit, and Lexy finished them off by tying raffia bows around the tops of the vases. While she scurried about getting every-thing set up, she noticed Nans and the ladies lin-gering by the mimosa table that was set up over near the part of the yard that sloped toward the pond. Lexy had purchased leg extenders for one side of the small table so that it would sit level even though the yard sloped. She wondered if the ladies' presence was because they were hatching their plan to get into the pond or if they were busy drinking mimosas.

Once she was convinced everything was set up perfectly, she managed to work her way around to the edge of the yard, where she had a view of the Pendletons'. No one was out thankfully, not even the dogs. She didn't need them barking and adding an annoying element to the brunch. She sidled around, looking through the trees to get a look at the gazebo. Was the blue tarp there? She edged over to an area from which she had a clear view.

The tarp was gone.

"Do you see the drone?" Ida was at her side, her hands shielding her eyes as she gazed over at the gazebo.

"No. Do you think it's in there?"

"Yesterday when I was over there, I saw the dogs digging in the corner under the wood. I was thinking maybe they had it there, but my controller didn't do any good. I need to get over there and dig."

Lexy turned to look at her. "I don't think today's a good day, Ida."

"Why not? Looks like nobody's home, and we're right here."

"Well, if they were home, it could cause a bit of a ruckus, and you wouldn't want to ruin my brunch here, would you?" Lexy asked.

Ida's eyes softened as they flicked from the Pendletons' yard to Lexy. She patted Lexy's arm. "No, of course not. I'll try to be on my best behavior."

And then she turned and walked away. Unfortunately, her words did not do much to make Lexy feel better. Ida's best behavior wasn't anything to feel optimistic about.

"Lexy, it looks lovely!" Caspian Kingsley and his wife Amanda stepped out from the house with wide smiles on their faces as they surveyed the area. Lexy flushed with pride, accepting the compliment. It did look pretty good, and the smell of bacon mixed with the earthy aroma of brewed coffee would surely perk even the groggiest guest up.

"Thank you." Lexy gestured toward the food stations. Hot foods were first. Scrambled eggs, sausages, and bacon in warming trays. Toast, scones, danish, and cinnamon buns were piled up on tiered servers set on a large table. Next to that, a giant fruit display boasted watermelon, pineapple, grapes, and berries. The last table rounded things out with yogurt, milk, and even some cereal for those who didn't want a big breakfast. "We're ready to serve."

"It's absolutely perfect." Amanda clapped her hands. "And the guests will be arriving any minute."

As if summoned by Amanda's prediction, Lexy heard the faint tinkle of the doorbell chiming inside the house, and Amanda fluttered off to greet her guests. Lexy rushed behind the serving station, ready to supervise and make sure everything went off without a hitch. The next several hours kept her busy making sure the food stations remained full and the guests had everything they needed. She even managed to hand out a few business cards.

To their credit, Nans and the ladies really did make themselves useful by circulating with little round trays loaded with bite-size pieces of Lexy's breakfast pastries. Everyone thought they were charming. *If they only knew they were really here trying to find a dead body*, she thought.

When the crowd started to dwindle, Lexy noticed Nans and the ladies edging closer to the pond. It didn't take long before they were down at the very edge, fumbling about in the weeds.

Had Ruth dragged her wetsuit down there?

Lexy certainly hoped she wasn't going to put it on and jump in. She was just about to head down there herself and pull them away when Ida leaned over and pointed at something at the water's edge.

"That's it! Evidence!" Ida yelled loud enough for the entire neighborhood to hear. "See it?"

Everyone that was left at the brunch was drawn by her words and came to the edge of the yard, peering over Lexy's shoulder. Lexy felt her earlier enthusiasm draining. The brunch had gone off perfectly so far, and she was sure people would be talking about her and recommending her catering service. Now she hoped that wouldn't be replaced by talk of her grandmother dragging a body out of the pond.

"I'll hold your arm, and you lean over and grab it," Nans said, confirming Lexy's worst fears that they'd found the body and were about to fish it out.

"You could fall in! Don't you think we should call the police?" Lexy yelled. All heads swiveled toward her.

"Police?" Caspian Kingsley had appeared beside her with a curious look on his face. "Why would we need the police? Those dogs aren't barking."

"I...umm... they said they found..." Lexy's gaze swiveled back to her grandmother and the ladies. Ida was leaning precariously over the edge of the pond. Nans and Ruth had hold of one of her arms, their heels dug into the sloping ground as they held her in place. Ida leaned over the swampy edge of the pond, her other arm outstretched to grab something that lay in the weeds.

"Got it!" Ida held her hand up. In it was a small gold object. Lexy was relieved it was just that and not a body part. But what was it? A piece of jewelry? A ring? Hopefully *not* attached to a finger.

Nans and Ruth hauled Ida back, and they bent their heads together to examine what Ida had in her hand.

The remaining brunch crowd was now leaning over, talking excitedly wondering what the crazy lady had. Lexy edged down the side of the yard. She was curious to see what they'd found. Maybe they were about to solve the case.

"Is it—"

"*Woof!*"

"*Yip!*"

"*Snarl!*"

"Hey, what are you doing?" Rupert Pendleton came charging across the yard behind the four Peekapoos. Nans, Ruth, Ida, and Helen turned in alarm, Ida clutching the piece of jewelry, which Lexy now saw was a gold ring.

"Uh oh," Nans said.

"We've got you now!" Ida held her hand up with the ring in it.

Rupert scrunched his face up. "What are you talking about?" His gaze flicked to Nans. "She's the one that's senile, right?"

"Senile as a sly fox," Ida said.

"What are you people doing in my yard?" Rupert glanced up at Kingsley. "Have these ladies been bothering you, too? They've been lurking around my place for the past week. I think we should have them arrested."

"I'll have you know, we are here on official business. We are catering an event for the Kingsleys." Nans gestured up the hill to where the tent and tables still stood, and everyone turned in that direction.

Lexy heard the Pendletons' squeaky sliding door open, and a woman's voice called out, "What's going on over there?"

Everyone swiveled back to see the new arrival. Lexy's heart skittered. Were Susan and Rupert onto them and going to confront them? But if so, what could they possibly do to them with all these witnesses?

"Oh, that's the ring I lost last summer. Wherever did you find it?" The woman reached out and snatched the ring from Ida's hand, looked it over, then slipped it on her finger. "Now, what in the world is going on here?"

But neither Nans, Ruth, Ida, Helen, or Lexy answered her. They were speechless, because the woman in front of them was Olive Pendleton, and she was very much alive.

Sixteen

"Well now, that's a fine how do you do," Ida said later on as they were piling out of Lexy's car at the Brook Ridge Falls Retirement Center.

"That was a quick jaunt to Europe," Nans said.

"*If* she was even there," Ida pointed out.

"Well, since she isn't the person we saw pushed, she could have left Saturday morning or earlier. Spent two days there and come back. It's doable," Helen said.

"But Rupert said she was napping Saturday afternoon," Ida said.

"He probably lied."

"She could have flown in overnight," Nans pointed out. "When I went to Italy, I flew overnight, slept right through, and woke up there the next day. She'd have three full days there and then fly back Tuesday night."

Ruth nodded. "This sure does put a damper on our investigation, though."

"What's Jack going to say?" Nans asked.

"I don't think he's going to be happy." Lexy pulled her cell phone out. "I'll text him so he doesn't waste any more time on this."

"Well, don't call him off completely," Nans said. "I'm certain we witnessed a murder through the drone, and that still needs to be investigated."

"Yeah, but *whose*?" Helen asked.

"I don't know. My money says whoever it was is in that pond." Ruth signaled for Lexy to pop the trunk, and she wrestled the wetsuit out of it. "I didn't get a chance to go in there today. Maybe we can go back tonight and I'll get a chance to go looking around."

"It's dark at night, Ruth. Are you gonna bring a big underwater flashlight?" Helen asked.

"And besides, who wants to see you in that wetsuit anyway? You'll scare the neighbors," Ida added.

Ruth fisted her hands on her hips. "Hey, I still look pretty good in this thing."

"We're not going to go back and jump in the pond," Nans said. "We need to go over the clues. We've obviously been looking at this from the wrong angle."

"You can say that again," Ida said sarcastically.

"I think we better stay away from the Pendletons," Lexy said. "We were lucky that the Kingsleys talked them out of calling the cops."

"I hope we didn't ruin your chances at getting other catering jobs."

Lexy's heart warmed at the genuine concern in Ida's voice. "I'm sure I'll be fine. Most of the people had already left, and Kingsley did say I had done a great job. Luckily, he didn't let your antics reflect badly on me."

"And hopefully we haven't gotten you into trouble with Jack either," Ruth said.

Lexy pressed her lips together. She didn't relish the idea of telling him that Olive Pendleton was still alive. He'd gone out on a limb to get information for them. But it wouldn't all be for nothing. After all, *someone* was dead, and *somebody* needed to get them justice.

"I'm sure he'll be fine. After all, somebody did die, right?" Lexy was starting to second-guess herself. She was sure no one could have survived that fall, but if Olive was alive, then *who* was the victim?

"Of course. We just have to figure out who it was that Rupert killed and why." Nans started walking toward the building. "And we need to get to that whiteboard and look at the clues from this new angle."

"It's obvious we need to look into the maid and the assistant. If one of them was the victim, then they would have been missing for several days now. Should be pretty easy to figure out which one," Helen said.

The whiteboard was still set up in Nans' dining room. She took her place in front of it, pointing at each clue in turn so that they could discuss them from this new perspective.

"So, our theory of Rupert having the affair with Susan and killing Olive to get her out of the way doesn't hold water now," Nans said.

"Maybe Rupert was having an affair, and *Olive* killed the person he was having the affair with," Ruth suggested.

Nans screwed up her face. "Her own sister?"

"But Rupert swung the bat. Why would he kill his lover?" Helen asked.

"Good question," Ida said.

"Or maybe he had a fight with the lover and killed her in the heat of passion!" Ida suggested.

"No. It was definitely premeditated. He got her on the balcony and then clonked her on the head. He had to have planned that out," Lexy said.

Nans looked at the whiteboard and sighed. "Maybe the whole theory about Rupert's affair was an erroneous assumption. This could be about the money."

"Are we even sure somebody *is* dead?" Ruth asked.

"Of course we are," Helen said. "No one could've survived that fall, and you saw the body lying there not moving a muscle."

"That's right." Nans tapped the marker on the whiteboard. "We just have to figure out who it was, and as Helen pointed out, it should be fairly easy once we figure out who has been missing for the last several days."

"We can already rule out Susan, because we found that note in the mailbox after the murder, and the fan club ladies saw her driving away from the house after the murder," Ida said.

"Right. Before this, we thought the killers were Susan and Rupert. Maybe it was Susan and Olive," Ruth suggested.

"But why?" Lexy asked. "What would their motive be?"

"Well, if they were as close as people say, Olive might've discovered Rupert was having the affair, and she had the sister help her kill the other woman," Ida said.

"Rupert had mud on his pants when we went over later that day from dumping the body in the pond, though." Helen said.

"I noticed that too," Lexy said. "But we just *assumed* that's what the mud was from. It's muddy over by the gazebo, too, and we know he's been working over there."

Nans shook her head. "I don't think the theory of Olive and Susan being the killers holds water, because Rupert would notice his lover was missing. No, there has to be another motive."

Ruth shrugged. "Then if it's not about love, it must be about money."

"Blackmail!" Ida said.

"Mildred did say that Rupert went in every other Tuesday and put a large sum of money into a cashier's check." Helen looked at Ruth. "Did Mildred happen to say who the check was made out to?"

Ruth pressed her lips together. "You know, I believe she said it was made out to cash."

"That's odd," Ida said. "Why wouldn't he just use the cash?"

"Maybe he didn't want to carry a big wad of it around. Maybe the blackmailer didn't want to get a thick envelope filled with money. That's a lot of money. Maybe the drop-off point was a post office box that wasn't large enough to hold it," Nans suggested.

Ruth tapped her index finger on her lips. "Those are all good theories. So if someone was blackmailing Rupert, then why?"

Ida snapped her fingers. "I've got it! Rupert *was* having an affair. Maybe with the sister, or the maid or the assistant. I don't know which one. But then someone else found out and started to blackmail him."

"You know, that makes perfect sense," Helen said. "Olive made the money with her books, and she had family money. Rupert didn't have any money of his own, so naturally he couldn't risk a divorce."

"Jack said their finances weren't that great, so Rupert would likely be left with nothing if he had to split from Olive," Lexy said.

"And knowing the way her parents were, they probably forced her to have a prenup so he'd get nothing in a divorce, especially if she could prove he was having an affair."

"But Rupert couldn't keep paying the blackmailer. Olive was bound to notice the money was missing sooner or later," Helen said.

"That's why he killed the blackmailer," Ruth added.

Nans added the words "maid" and "Connie" to the suspect list on the whiteboard. "Now if we could just figure out who he was having the affair with, that would eliminate one person. The dead person has to be the other one."

Nans stood back from the whiteboard. "Okay then. We know we need to find more information on the maid, and we need to talk to the assistant, Connie. Now who else should we talk to?"

"The busybody neighbor, Mrs. Jensen," Ruth suggested.

"Good idea." Nans wrote Mrs. Jensen's name on the whiteboard.

"What about Susan's son?" Helen asked. "I know Caspian Kingsley said they were estranged, but she had put the letter in her mailbox, and I can't help but think maybe they were reconciling. It seems like Susan might be mixed up in something with Rupert. Maybe the son knows something about it?"

"It might even be the reason they were estranged," Ruth added.

"Does anyone remember the son's name?" Nans asked.

"I do," Ida said. "Brent Chambers, 121 Forest Ave., Oakdale, Kentucky."

"Wow, that's pretty good," Lexy said.

Ida puffed up with pride. "Thank you. My mind is like a steel trap on account'a all that cypher work I did in my younger days." Ida had a knack for deciphering codes, and Jack had actually used her a few times to decode things for the police cases.

"Oh, that reminds me!" Ida swung her purse up onto the table and rummaged inside. "This might give us some clues." She pulled out an envelope and slapped it on the table. It was from Brook Ridge Bank. Susan's latest bank statement.

Nans frowned at it. "What is that?"

Ida's eyes gleamed mischievously. "When we were at Susan's and the mailman came, I couldn't help but do a little sleight-of-hand, and I pilfered this from the pile before stuffing the rest in her mailbox."

Helen sucked in a breath. "Ida! That's against the law!"

"Law schmaw." Ida slid the envelope into the middle of the table. "Come on, I know you guys are dying to see what's in here. Her finances could give us a big clue."

Ruth eyed the envelope uncertainly. "Well, I suppose it would be okay. I mean, the police could get access to this information if they had probable cause. So if Jack could actually investigate this case, we'd be able to know about her financial activities. We're simply circumventing that just a little bit."

"And if we steamed it open and then glued it back, no one would ever know," Helen suggested.

Nans sighed. "Okay. Fine." She cast an uncertain glance at Lexy.

Lexy shrugged. "I'm not gonna tell Jack."

Ida snatched the envelope up from the table and ran into the kitchen. She turned the teakettle on, tapping her fingernail on the stove impatiently as she waited for it to heat up. When it whistled, she ran the envelope through the steam, melting the glue and curling the edges of the flap until it popped open.

She slid the statement out, her eyes growing wide as she read it. "Look. Right here. This is the proof."

She turned the statement to face them, pointing out two lines, each with a ten-thousand-dollar cash withdrawal. "She made two big withdrawals this week. You know what that means."

"Blackmail," Ruth said.

"If that's true, then Rupert wasn't the only one being blackmailed. Susan was being blackmailed along with him, which would give her just as much reason to want the blackmailer dead."

"And who better to notice they were having an affair and put the screws to them but the maid who would see everything that was going on in the house?" Ida said.

Seventeen

"We always knew the killer must've had an accomplice. I don't think they could have disposed of the body in that pond so quickly otherwise," Nans said as they rushed out of the building on their way to Lexy's car.

Nans had called the cleaning company, pretending to be a neighbor of the Pendletons. She'd buttered them up by saying how wonderfully clean the Pendletons' home was and that it had passed her strict white glove inspection; then she expressed an interest in having the same person clean her house. But before she would enter into any kind of agreement, she would have to have her "people" do a background check.

The company was eager enough to give the woman's name out—Amelia Little—and a few keystrokes later, Ruth discovered she lived in an apartment on the other side of town, to which they were now headed.

"Listen, guys, I'd love to spend all day investigating, but I have a business to run," Lexy said.

"Oh, don't worry, dear, we'll help you with the business afterwards. You know five pairs of hands are better than one," Ruth said.

Lexy angled the rearview mirror to peer back at Ruth's eager face. It was nice of them to offer to help, but Lexy wasn't sure how much help they actually would be. Though she did love investigating, she needed to pay attention to her bread and butter—the bakery business.

"Just this one trip, dear." Nans gave her "the look" from the passenger seat, and Lexy snapped her attention back onto the road. "After that, Ruth can drive us around in the Olds."

Lexy frowned as she navigated the streets. The idea of Ruth driving them around was unsettling. Maybe she could just text Cassie and see if she could watch the bakery for the rest of the day. Their part-time girl Holly was helping out all day and had been in early, since Lexy and Cassie were busy with the brunch. The bakery should be well covered, but she still hated spending so much time away from it.

"So now we're back to Susan and Rupert being the killers. I knew we were on the right track all along," Ida said as she stared out the side window.

"Right. We just got the victim wrong," Helen said.

"I was kind of surprised to see that Susan has so much money in the bank. Judging by that little house she lives in, I thought she didn't have much. Maybe she inherited a lot from her folks. But then if she did, why doesn't Olive seem to have as much money?" Ida asked.

"It takes a lot to run that big house the Pendletons have, plus Kingsley said Susan invested her money wisely." Nans twisted around in her seat to look at the ladies in the back, who all nodded. "Maybe Olive wasn't as wise with her investments."

"This is the street coming up," Ruth said, her eyes locked on the GPS display on her phone.

Lexy turned onto the street. It was filled with two-story older apartments on small patches of land barely larger than the building itself. All the homes were nicely maintained and the yards neatly kept. Though the parked cars were older, none of them were junkers. It was the type of neighborhood where younger people with decent jobs would rent before they were able to buy their own homes.

"Pull in here." Ruth pointed to a parking spot at the side of the road. "The house is that red one over there."

149

Lexy did as told, and they all piled out of the car and gathered on the porch of the red house. Nans rang the bell.

"If Amelia is our victim, she's not going to answer." Ida pressed her face against the window then jumped back as a figure came from the back of the house toward the door.

A dark-haired woman of about twenty-five stood in the doorway, an inquisitive look on her face. "Can I help you?"

"We're looking for Amelia Little," Nans said. Amelia was a blonde, so unless she'd recently dyed her hair, the woman at the door was not her.

The woman's eyes drifted among them. "And what is this in regard to?"

"Oh, I'm so sorry, dear, we forgot to introduce ourselves. We are the ladies' auxiliary, and we heard from Olive Pendleton how wonderful Amelia was at cleaning, and we were hoping to secure her services." Nans peered over the woman's shoulder. "Is she home?"

"Olive Pendleton sent you? Isn't she nice?" the woman said. "Oh, I'm Amelia's sister."

"Yes, Olive is very nice," Nans said. "Is Amelia home?"

"No, I'm so sorry. Didn't Olive tell you? She sent Amelia on a little trip. Well, it was all very quick. I guess she got the tickets and couldn't use them and wanted to reward Amelia for her hard work."

"A trip?" I asked. "What kind of trip?"

"To the Bahamas. Isn't that cool? I just wish they'd had two tickets instead of one." The sister leaned against the doorjamb.

"So she went by herself?" Lexy asked.

"Yep, left on Friday, I believe it was. She left me a note."

"So you didn't see her leave?" Nans said.

The sister's brow furrowed. "No, why?"

"Oh, no reason," Nans said. "So your sister must be close to the Pendletons. Both Olive and Rupert?"

"I don't know about that. But Mrs. Pendleton is really nice to her. She gives Amelia a lot of her old clothes. They're the same size. But they don't have a lot of money, which is why this trip was a big surprise."

"I'll bet it was," Ida said.

The sister shot Ida a confused look then said, "She'll be back tomorrow if you guys want to come back then." She stepped back from the door and started to close it. "Have a great day."

They turned away from the door. As they walked down the steps, Ida whispered, "Nice my patootie. Maybe Rupert and Susan somehow left a note that the sister *thought* was from Amelia to explain why she wasn't around."

"The victim was wearing the maroon sweater that you saw on the back of the book jacket," Lexy pointed out.

Ruth snapped her fingers. "That's right! I had forgotten about that, and that girl just told us Olive gave her old clothes to Amelia."

"A maid would have access to all kinds of household secrets. She could find hidden love letters or witness secret rendezvouses," Helen said.

"And a maid would certainly be happy to increase her meager income with some blackmail money," Ida added.

"We should look into Amelia's finances and see if she's made any big deposits lately," Nans said.

"Now, let's not forget the basics. We've already established means, and we're pretty sure we know the motive, but we need to establish opportunity," Ruth said.

"That's right. We need to establish that Amelia was at the Pendletons' house Saturday morning," Ida said.

"We need someone that keeps an eagle eye on the neighborhood, and I know just the person," Helen said. "Mrs. Jensen."

Eighteen

Nans, Ruth, Ida, and Helen talked Lexy into swinging by *the Cup and Cake* to pick up some pastries on their way to Mrs. Jensen's. At the bakery, Cassie had things well under control. She'd put everything away from the Kingsleys' event earlier that morning and had resupplied the bakery case out front with fresh baked goods.

A handful of customers sat at the café tables by the window, sipping coffee and eating blueberry scones and coffee cake. Lexy was both pleased and dismayed to discover that the bakery could run just fine without her.

Nans and the ladies stood in front of the glass bakery case, picking out various treats for Lexy to put in the box. When they were done, she tied it with pink-striped bakery twine, and they piled back into the car with Ida balancing the box on her lap in the back seat.

"I hope this lady gives us some good gossip," Ruth said.

"Don't let me forget to look for the drone while we're there," Ida said as she pushed the string to one side so she could pry up the top of the bakery box. "Oh look, there's a broken cannoli in here. You don't want to present this to Mrs. Jensen. Might make it look like you put out shoddy goods. I'll just have to eat it."

Lexy parked in front of Mrs. Jensen's house, where the busybody was obviously staring out the window through the shade. And as they got out and started up the brick walkway, the shade snapped shut, and a few seconds later the door opened, giving them their first glimpse of the elderly woman. She wore a flowered housecoat. Her thinning gray hair was cut short, her hazel eyes were bright with excitement, and her cheeks were flushed. She seemed eager to have someone to talk to, especially people that were carrying a bakery box.

"I've seen you ladies here before, haven't I?" Mrs. Jensen asked, her eyes flicking from Nans to the bakery box.

"Why yes, we've been coming around the neighborhood with these baked goods from my granddaughter's bakery, *the Cup and Cake*." Nans grabbed the box from Ida and held it up. "She recently catered a brunch over at the Kingsleys'."

"Oh, I saw that going on." Mrs. Jensen pushed the door open wider, inviting them in. "Not much happens in this neighborhood that gets by me."

Nans, Ruth, Ida, and Helen exchanged excited looks as they followed the woman down a hallway past a grand set of stairs and into a sparkling-clean old-fashioned kitchen with hardwood floors and whitewashed cabinets. Mrs. Jensen set the bakery box down on her marble countertop, pulled out a crystal serving plate, and started arranging the pastries in a neat circle.

"Do you ladies like coffee or tea? Oh, where are my manners?" She wiped her fingers off on a kitchen towel and stuck out her right hand. "My name is Rita Jenkins."

They all shook hands, put in their orders for coffee, and sat at the large wooden kitchen table while Rita boiled water, took out fancy napkins, and put little crystal plates on the table in front of them.

Rita sat down and picked a chocolate scone off the plate. The ladies had patiently waited for her to choose first, which Lexy found unusually patient of them, especially Ida, who usually couldn't wait to dig in. Apparently eating the cannoli on the way over had given her some restraint.

"This is delicious," Rita mumbled around a mouthful of scone.

Helen nodded knowingly and winked at Lexy, obviously proud that she'd come up with the suggestion for the chocolate scones in the first place.

"Thank you," Lexy said. "Have you been to my bakery? It's right downtown."

Rita shook her head. "I'm sorry. I don't get out much. But I'll check it out the next time I'm in town."

"This is a lovely home," Helen said. "Do you live here alone?"

Rita's face turned sad. "Yes. My Henry died a few years back, and it's just me and Jake."

"Jake?"

"My cat." Rita nodded toward the corner, and Lexy turned to see an orange-and-white cat hunkered down, watching them curiously.

"I'll bet Jake knows all the neighbors we should visit with our baked goods," Nans said.

"I know all the neighbors," Rita said. "You should go to the Harringtons' next door, and then three doors down is Bert and Iona Reynolds. They have a lot of parties. You should check them."

"What about the Pendletons?" Nans asked.

Rita frowned. "They do have parties, but they're a little odd."

"That's what I heard," Ruth said. "But she's an author, and they are known to be eccentric."

Rita pursed her lips. "Hmmm."

"I take it you don't approve," Ida said.

"It's just that there are some strange goings-on over there. And there's a gaggle of old ladies that hang around watching the place. At first I thought they were casing the joint. I almost called the police."

"The fan club," Nans said.

Rita nodded. "That's right. I found that out later. And then there was the strange device flying around in the yard the other day."

Ida sat up straight in her seat. "You saw a strange device? What happened to it?"

"I don't know. I saw it fly down the street, but I can only see so much from here." Rita looked at the cat. "Jake went crazy."

"Why, that was—" Helen started, but Nans kicked her under the table. Judging by the gleam in Nans' eye, Lexy figured she'd had a brainstorm.

"I think I heard about that ... that was Saturday, right? The morning the cleaning people come. I have the same cleaning lady that Olive does, and I think she mentioned it, as she was there that morning."

Rita's forehead creased. "No, not that day. I mean, the cleaning lady *does* usually come on

Saturday, but every other week. That was her off week. She wasn't there the morning I saw the drone. Olive's sister, Susan, was there—she'd come very early that day and brought the little black dog...and then the assistant came."

Nans leaned forward. "Olive's assistant? She was there the morning you saw the drone? Are you sure?"

"Yes, of course. Her name is Connie Davis. She lives right on the street behind me, and I'm positive she was there that morning."

Nineteen

They'd bowed out of Rita Jensen's kitchen as soon as she'd dropped the bomb about Connie. They left the pastries behind, much to Ida's dismay, and drove one street over. Connie lived on the street that was the border between the wealthy neighborhood and the section of town where the older homes had been all turned into apartments. Her house was a modest 1940s style. They parked in front of it and bustled up the walkway onto the porch.

"Look!" Nans pointed to several days' worth of newspapers piled up on the welcome mat. "She hasn't been here in days!"

"Do you think she's the murder victim?" Ruth asked.

"But what about the maid? I thought they made up the thing about her going on a trip so no one would miss her," Helen said.

160

"Maybe they sent the maid on a trip so she wouldn't see them murder Connie," Ida suggested.

"But why would they need to do that? She didn't come on Saturday—that was her off day," Lexy said.

"Good point," Nans said.

Ida looked at the mailbox. "Maybe they got the weeks confused. That happens to me sometimes."

"Either way, we've got to look into Connie's finances and see if she had any big deposits. If she did, then that means she's the blackmailer, and—"

"Aren't you the nosy ladies that were in my pond?"

They whirled around to see Olive Pendleton standing at the bottom of the steps, her brows quirked up. "What are you people doing here?"

"Umm...we came to visit Connie," Nans stuttered.

"You know Connie?" Olive looked like she didn't believe them.

"Yes. Well, sort of. We met her at a writers' conference," Ida said.

"Oh really? Which one?"

"Well, it doesn't really matter. There's been so many I can hardly remember. We're huge fans of your writing." Lexy figured she might as well try to butter Olive up.

Olive blushed. "Oh, you are? How lovely. Then you know Connie is my assistant."

"We do. We actually thought she was you at the convention," Ruth said.

Olive leaned toward them and lowered her voice. "Truth is, I send her as me sometimes. I don't like to go to them very much, and she just makes an appearance and people think I'm there. In fact, that's where she is right now. At Murder-Con. I just came by to pick up newspapers and mail."

"Oh, I see. So she's not home then?" Ida asked.

"No. As I just explained she's at a convention." Olive looked at Ida as if she were dim witted, then recognition bloomed on her face and she leaned forward toward Nans. "Oh, is that the senile one Rupert told me about?"

"Yes. Poor thing," Nans said, ignoring Ida's glare.

"So you've talked to Connie at the convention then?" Helen asked.

"Talked to her? A little bit. We don't usually talk much. She just goes off and pretends to be me a few times, and then she's free to do as she wishes."

"Sounds like a pretty good gig," Ruth said.

Olive laughed. "Yes, I guess it is." Olive stepped up on the porch, bent over, and started picking up the newspapers. A red leather note-book fell out of her pocket, a green pamphlet sticking out of the top. Lexy noticed the Happy House Cleaner logo on top of the pamphlet.

"Is that from the cleaning service that every-one here uses?" Lexy asked. "I was thinking about using them."

"What?" Olive looked down at the pamphlet. "Oh, yes. This is my writer's journal. I carry it with me at all times. Sometimes I shove pamphlets and notes in there. I was going to call them to get a new cleaner. Rupert is unhappy with the girl we use now."

Nans' brows shot up. "Oh really? Who is it? I daresay we wouldn't want to use her if she is no good."

Olive's expression turned guarded. "I don't re-ally want to name names. She did a fine job...and it's just that Rupert... Well, I don't feel right talk-ing bad about her."

"Oh, sure. We understand." Lexy eyed Nans and the ladies.

Olive smiled then opened up the little mailbox beside the door and pulled out four envelopes. One was a pretty robin's-egg blue, while the oth-ers looked like random bills. One might've even been a bank statement, and Lexy could see Ida eyeing it enviously, probably wishing she'd gotten the chance to open the mailbox before Olive had appeared on the scene.

"I heard you were in Paris this past week." Helen gave Olive a sly wink. "Or was that Connie?"

"No, that one I went to on my own. With my sister, of course."

"Of course. Do you take your sister on a lot of trips?"

"Sometimes. She's a little shy and doesn't like to travel much though."

"It's nice that you and Rupert take care of her like that," Nans said.

Olive's forehead creased. "Well, she is my sister."

"How is your gazebo project coming?" Ruth asked. "Will you be cleaning out the pond once that's done?"

"Rupert is working on the gazebo." Olive's lips pressed together. "He seems averse to cleaning out the pond. You seem to be awfully interested in it. Why is that?"

"Oh, I'm somewhat of an environmentalist, and I hate to see the local waterways choked off. You know, if you keep letting that pond grow over like that, it will dry up completely. It's home to millions of frogs, salamanders, and fish. I'd hate to think of what would happen to them." Ruth shook her head. "You know, I could get my suit on and go in there and clean out some of the vegetation."

Olive's face puckered as if she were picturing Ruth in her wetsuit. "I don't think that will be necessary, but to tell you the truth, I haven't really thought about the impact of having the pond so overgrown. Maybe I should consider having it cleaned out...by a *professional*." Olive shrugged. "I'm a big lover of animals, you know. Of course I have my beloved Peekapoos, but I love all creatures, even the frogs in the pond. I wouldn't want them to come to harm. It's expensive having a big property like that, but with my new book release, I may just have the money to do it."

Olive turned toward the steps and then looked at them expectantly. "Well, now you know that Connie's not here, so..."

"Right." Nans started down the steps. "We'll be seeing you later then."

"Alrighty." Olive watched them all the way to the sidewalk, and then she walked down the steps, crossed the street, and headed toward her house.

"Looks like she's on foot," Ruth said.

"Yeah, I wonder where her red Cadillac is. Is it somewhere in a remote spot in the woods? You don't think Rupert is still planning on doing something to her, do you?" Lexy asked.

"I don't know, but it seems like the poor thing is clueless. Obviously she has no idea Rupert and her sister are fooling around behind her back," Helen said.

"Nor any idea that there is a dead body in her pond," Ida added. "I mean, you saw the look on her face when she thought about cleaning it out. She seemed genuinely concerned about the frogs and salamanders. Clearly she was not averse to the idea."

Helen glanced back at Connie's empty house. "Do you think Connie is really at the convention?"

"I'm not sure. Apparently Olive thinks she is, but if Rupert did away with her..." Ida's voice trailed off.

"I'm not sure Connie was the victim. Did you see that pamphlet for the cleaning service? Rupert might have been pretending that Amelia's cleaning wasn't up to par so that Olive wouldn't ask any questions when Amelia didn't show up again. He's cleverly covering all his tracks," Lexy said.

"I just wish you would stop telling everyone I'm senile. I am not senile," Ida said.

"Sorry, Ida, but you know, that actually would come in handy. It would give us excuses for you to do all kinds of things that might help us on the cases. You can act senile pretty easily, can't you?" Nans asked, and Ruth and Helen laughed.

Ida scowled at them. "You think you're so smart. You tell me, now *who* is our victim? The maid is missing *and* Connie is missing."

"Olive said Connie was at a convention. That should be easy enough to check," Helen said.

"Really? She's at the convention as Olive. Would she be registered as Olive or Connie or someone else entirely?"

"And even if she is? Can we be assured that she's really actually there?" Ruth asked. "Rupert could have gone out and registered her to make it *seem* like she was there and then driven back here."

"All the more reason to look into Connie's finances," Nans said.

"Yeah, too bad I didn't get to the mailbox before Olive did." Ida glanced back at the house, a scowl on her face.

"How are we going to look at her finances without official access?" Helen asked.

They all turned to Lexy.

"Oh no. I don't think Jack can get police resources involved on this. He's probably already a little upset with us that we led him on the wild goose chase of Olive Pendleton's murder. We need to tread carefully now," Lexy said.

"Okay. If we can't look into her finances that way, then how about we attack it from a different angle?" Ruth asked.

"What do you mean?" Helen asked.

"Well, we certainly can't ask Rupert or Susan, but there's one person who might know something about what's going on," Ruth said. "We saw that letter in Susan's mailbox addressed to her son. If she was trying to reconcile with him, she might've let something slip."

"I don't see that we have many other options, so I guess it's worth a phone call," Nans said.

"In the meantime, I'll look into this convention to see if I can find evidence that Connie really was there," Ruth said.

"Good idea." Nans looked in the direction of the Pendleton house, her forehead creased in worry. "I just hope the person we saw fall from the balcony is the *only* murder victim. We have two people that are missing."

"Once you've killed one time, it's easier to do it a second," Ruth said. "And there could be a lot of evidence at the Pendleton house from the first murder. What if Connie or the maid stumbled across some of it and Rupert had to silence her?"

"Worse yet," Ida said, "what if *Olive* stumbles across that evidence or asks too many questions?

Rupert could get anxious. And if he gets too anxious, Olive could be his next victim."

Twenty

Where to?" Lexy asked after they were belted into their seats in her car. "I need to get to the bakery. I can't leave Cassie to do all the work, especially since there's the added cleanup duties from the Kingsley brunch."

"Oh, we can help with that," Nans said. "Ruth can dig into that writers' conference on her iPad and also get me Susan's son's phone number. I can call right from the bakery."

Lexy didn't really want the ladies' help. Their idea of helping was usually to sit at the front table in the corner and eat her pastries for free. But she wanted to stay up to date with the investigation, and it couldn't really hurt anything to have them at the bakery.

"Okay, fine, but don't eat all my chocolate-frosted brownies like you did last time." Lexy swung the car around and headed toward *the Cup and Cake,* with Ruth tapping away on the iPad the entire time.

"I didn't find anything about Olive—or Connie, rather—other than to say she was at the conference. There's no pictures or anything, and she wasn't on any boards or panels, so I'm afraid my research is inconclusive," Ruth said as they all piled out of Lexy's car and into the back door of the bakery. Cassie was in the kitchen, working on a Boston cream pie. Her eyes widened and her face cracked into a smile when she saw Nans and the ladies.

"Hey, ladies, what a great surprise. I didn't know you were coming to visit today." She winked at Lexy.

"Oh, we're just here to help out. We took up some of Lexy's time, and we know you girls are extra busy with that catering job this morning, so we figured we'd come in and lend a hand," Nans said.

Cassie's gaze flicked from Nans to Lexy. "The café tables need to be cleaned, and the pastry case needs to be stocked with these cookies." Cassie pointed to a tray of flower-shaped cookies decorated in colorful blue, pink, and purple frosting.

Nans, Ruth, Ida, and Helen reached into the box of food-service gloves, each pulling out a pair and putting them on. Ida grabbed the tray of cookies. "Don't worry, we'll do a good job," she assured them as they turned and hurried toward the front of the bakery.

Happy to be among the familiar sights, smells, and sounds of the bakery, Lexy got to work putting away the things they'd used at the Kingsley brunch. She boxed up some of the leftover pastries to bring to the food shelter later on and made a special box for Nans and the ladies to take back to the retirement center.

"Things went well at the Kingsleys'," Cassie said as they worked side by side in the kitchen.

"Very good...until Ida almost went swimming in the pond," Lexy said.

"That was kind of funny," Cassie said. "Are you making any headway on that case? It sure was a shocker that Olive Pendleton was still alive. I thought she was your murder victim."

"Yeah, no kidding. But we did see *someone* get murdered. We have a couple of ideas who else it could be."

"But didn't you see it on video? How come you thought it was Olive?"

"It looked like her. Turns out she has an assistant that could be a stunt double, and the maid is blond with a similar hairstyle. The video was kind of grainy, and Ida was a little jittery. We only ever saw the victim from the back."

"Oh, I could see how you could make that mistake. Did you tell Jack yet?" Cassie peered up at her over the Boston cream pie.

"I texted him. I'm not supposed to call him during the workday unless it's an emergency."

"John said that Jack was doing some extra work looking into this. He's not going to be happy."

"No kidding. But it was an honest mistake, and somebody did die, so there *is* a murder to investigate."

The bells over the door chimed, signaling the entrance of a customer. Cassie nodded toward the front. "Your turn."

Out in front, Nans and the ladies had cleaned off the bistro tables, stocked the cookies in the display case, and were now sitting at one of the tables with various brownies, scones, and cupcakes laid out in front of them, as well as steaming cups of coffee and tea.

"We can wait on the customers, too, Lexy," Ruth said hopefully.

No way did she want Nans and the ladies waiting on customers. "That's okay. I'll get them."

Lexy turned to the middle-aged couple that had come in. "Can I help you?"

"We'd like a dozen cupcakes. Can we pick them out?"

"Of course."

Lexy opened the back door of the case and pulled out the cupcakes one by one as the woman picked them out. She placed them in a white bakery box, which she tied up with twine and brought over to the cash register once they were done.

After the couple had paid and were out the door, Nans motioned her over. "I'm going to call Susan's son now. Do you want to listen in? I've already figured out a good angle to get him to talk."

Lexy glanced out at the sidewalk. It was not a busy time of day. The bakery was usually busiest at lunch time and after people got out of work. This would be a perfect time for Nans to call, with little risk of customers coming in and wondering what in the world they were doing.

"What's the number, Ruth?" Nans asked.

Ruth rattled off a number, and Nans dialed then held the phone a little bit away from her ear while everyone leaned in to try to hear the conversation.

"Hello?" The son's voice came out of Nans' phone.

"Hi, is this Brent Chambers?" Nans asked.

"Yes." The voice was cautious.

"Oh, good. This is Helen Smith. I'm a reporter at the *Brook Ridge Falls Chronicle*, and we're doing a piece on family members of famous local personalities."

"I think you might have the wrong number. I live in Kentucky."

"I know that, dear, but your aunt, Olive Pendleton, is a local celebrity, and I spoke with your mother, Susan, and now I could really use your input to my article."

"You talked to my mom?"

"Yes..." Nans paused. "I know you're having some difficulties, but I think things are going to work out."

Brent snorted. "Work out? I don't think so."

"What do you mean? Why just the other day when I spoke to Susan, she was mailing you a letter."

"Yeah, a letter telling me to stop contacting her." Brent's voice turned suspicious. "And why are you asking about this anyway? If you talked to my mother, you would know she doesn't want to talk to me. And just what does this have to do with my weird aunt Olive anyway?"

"So you think she's weird, too, huh?" Nans said. "She's known to be very eccentric, and her husband doesn't help much."

"Yeah, I'll say. They have my mom turned against me, I'm afraid."

"Oh, that's terrible, dear. You must be awfully upset. What happened?" Nans' voice was sympathetic, but her eyes held an eager glint as if she'd found a little chink in his armor that she could work away at and hopefully get more information.

"We had a stupid falling out over an old girlfriend I had years ago. We hadn't talked in almost five years when I contacted her trying to reconcile. Apparently since I left, she's spent more and more time with Olive and Rupert. I guess she doesn't need me anymore."

The ladies exchanged a look, and Lexy knew what they were thinking. What Brent didn't know was that apparently Susan had been spending a lot more time with Rupert than she had with Olive.

"I'm sure that's not true, dear. A mother always needs her son," Nans soothed.

"Well, apparently not my mother, because my mother is on an extended trip in Europe. She sent me a picture of her and Olive and told me in no uncertain terms that she would be incommunicado. I'm not stupid. I can take a hint."

"So you're not even going to keep trying to reconcile?" Nans asked.

"It seems pointless. She's refusing to talk to me, and the last letter made it pretty clear that she was still angry."

"But that won't last forever."

"Well, the original fight was pretty bad. She even changed her will... but that's not why I'm trying to reconcile with her. I don't care about the money."

"Of course not, dear. Then why are you trying to reconcile?"

"She's my mom!" Brent's voice took on a sheepish tone. "And, well, she was right about the girl."

"I see," Nans said. "Moms usually are."

Brent chuckled. "Yes, I realize that now that I'm older. Maybe things will work out. I just don't know if Aunt Olive is such a great influence."

Nans' brows shot up. "Oh? Why do you say that?"

"It's nothing bad, just that my mom doesn't have a very strong personality. She can be easily persuaded to do things, and Olive and Rupert are...well they're a little odd. I just don't want Mom to get into something that she can't get out of."

Ruth snorted and muttered under her breath, "Too late for that."

"So, as you can see, I don't really have much information about what it's like to have a local celebrity in the family. I've been out of town for years. So unfortunately, I don't think I have anything to add to your article."

"Well, thank you for your time," Nans said. "And I hope things work out with your mom."

Nans hung up the phone, a sad look on her face. "I didn't have the heart to tell him that his mother is right here in town."

"And the suspect in a murder investigation," Ida added.

"Seems weird that she would tell him she's in Europe," Ruth said.

"I bet Rupert put her up to it. It sounds like Susan can be easily manipulated, and Rupert wouldn't want Brent to come sniffing around," Lexy said.

Ruth tapped her index finger against her pursed lips. "Another thing he said bothered me. He implied he'd been written out of Susan's will, which means Olive was probably written in."

"Which means Rupert is probably after that money, because it's fairly obvious he doesn't have any, and I'm beginning to doubt whether Olive does either."

"Yeah, but how is he going to do that? I'm sure that if Susan wrote Brent out of the will, she probably made Olive her beneficiary."

"There's only one other way for Rupert to get the money. He'd have to marry Susan or somehow convince her to make him the beneficiary," Helen said.

"And if he was going to marry her, that would mean he would have to *not* be married to Olive," Lexy pointed out.

"And there's only two ways for him to accomplish that." Ida paused dramatically. "Divorce her or kill her."

Twenty-One

Lexy drove home that night with a feeling of dread weighing down her stomach. She hadn't heard back from Jack after texting him that Olive Pendleton was still alive. Would he be mad at her? She needed his help now more than ever, because all indications were that Olive could be in danger. They had to figure out how to get some evidence into the hands of the police so a real investigation could be done soon.

She walked in the door to the smell of pizza and the exuberant greeting of Sprinkles. Jack came in from the kitchen.

"So your murder victim wasn't really murdered, huh?" Jack dropped a kiss on her forehead, and relief flooded through her.

"Yeah, sorry about that. You're not mad?"

"No, I'm not mad. Though I will say it is a little bit unusual. But you still did witness a murder, right?"

"Yes. We just assumed it was Olive because it was at her house. But we uncovered some new clues today that might shed some light on things."

"Let's discuss them over pizza," Jack said. "I got your favorite—hamburger, green onion, and pepper."

Lexy's stomach grumbled. "Thanks! I'm starving."

Jack went into the kitchen and got the pizza, talking to her over his shoulder as he went. "How did your catering job at the Kingsleys' go?"

"It went off almost without a hitch. Except for the part where Nans, Ruth, Ida, and Helen almost fell into the Pendletons' pond."

Jack reappeared with paper plates, napkins, a roll of paper towels, and the pizza, all of which he deposited on the coffee table. While devouring a piece of gooey, salty, cheesy pizza, Lexy gave him the rundown on the Kingsleys' catered party, as well as the clues they'd spent the rest of the day following up on.

Jack picked up a second piece, folding it in half and shoving the pointed end into his mouth. "It sounds like Susan's son was a dead end. You already knew everything that he told you. You knew Susan had money, and since the son is in Kentucky and hasn't talked to Susan in years, it's unlikely he knows anything."

"The assistant could be the likely victim...or the maid."

"Is Rupert manipulative and controlling?"

Lexy thought back. Was he? He had seemed aggressive with the way he'd charged out after them, but Olive didn't seem to be any slouch in that department, either. She didn't seem like the type that would let a man control her. Then again, it was hard to tell, not having seen them together other than that one time at the edge of the pond. "I'm not really sure. Why do you ask?"

"If he's the controlling type, he might have pretended he was taking Connie to the convention. Or he might have manipulated things so that Olive thought Connie went there. It would be easy enough to do if he has her trust."

"Good point. And then Olive would think Connie was at the convention, so it would be perfectly normal that she wouldn't be coming over to assist her. Rupert might have taken the charade as far as even having Olive pick up Connie's mail."

"Devious."

"But what about the maid?"

"That's the other angle you need to investigate. Your theory about Rupert wanting to hire another maid because he didn't want Olive to ask questions about Amelia could be a good one. If Amelia *is* the victim, she's obviously not going to show up and clean the house. Rupert could be trying to circumvent any questions by explaining why she's not coming in advance. But I thought the maid was younger. And you seemed to think it was Olive in that video."

"Well, we didn't get a good look. We only saw the back of her head, and she was wearing an old-lady sweater. But Amelia's sister said that Olive gave Amelia some of her old clothes. So she could literally have been wearing Olive's sweater. And the other thing is that I think we just assumed it was Olive because it was her house."

"So either way, it seems like one of these unfortunate ladies saw something she shouldn't have seen going on between Rupert and Susan and then tried to take advantage of it by blackmailing them," Jack said.

"Right. So I can't really feel too bad for them, though they didn't deserve to be murdered," Lexy said.

Sprinkles came over and nudged herself in between Jack and Lexy on the couch. As Lexy scratched Sprinkles behind the ears, a pang of sympathy for her fellow pet lover Olive Pendleton surfaced. She hated to think of how hurt Olive would be when the truth came out about Rupert and Susan, not to mention the dead person in her pond.

"We did mention the pond to Olive, and she seemed like she might want to get it cleaned out. But if Rupert's controlling like you said, he probably won't allow it. Though it would make it easy if they did, since then the body would turn up," Lexy said.

"Yeah. Looks like we're going to have to find the body a different way. We need an official reason to question Olive and Rupert. We need a reason for the police to be on that property. And what better reason than a missing person?"

"Right! How are we going to do that?" Lexy asked.

Jack petted Sprinkles behind the other ear. "I think the thing to do is to figure out who the victim is. If Connie is supposed to be at the conference, you guys could go out to the conference and verify. Or you could go to the Bahamas and try to find the maid. Maybe if you could prove that one of them was missing, we could file a missing persons report and get an investigation going."

"Wait a minute! The sister said Amelia was coming back tomorrow. It would be a lot easier to check up on her than go all the way to that convention."

"Well then, it sounds like that's what you should do. First thing *tomorrow*." Jack pulled her up from the couch. "For tonight, I have a special undercover assignment for you," he said as he led her upstairs.

Twenty-Two

The next day, Lexy called Nans on her way to the bakery. "I talked to Jack last night and went over all our clues."

"Was he mad about Olive still being alive?" Nans' voice was hesitant.

"No. Not really."

"So he still believes there was a murder?"

"Yes. In fact, he had a good suggestion. He said that if we could prove that either Connie or Amelia were missing, we might be able to put in a missing persons report."

"We could? But doesn't that need to be done by a family member?"

"I'm not sure. But it's a lot easier to check into where Amelia is. Her sister said she should be coming back, and if she's not back, then maybe we can get the sister to put in the report."

Lexy pulled into her parking spot behind the bakery. She had a lot to do at the bakery this morning but was also anxious to investigate Amelia's whereabouts.

"If we can file a missing persons report, then Jack said the police will have an official reason to go over to the Pendletons'," Lexy added.

"Brilliant!"

Lexy heard the sounds of Nans covering the mouthpiece of her phone and then her muffled voice. "No, Ida, not missing drone report. A missing persons report. Don't worry, we'll find your drone." Then she came back to the phone. "Ida is getting nervous about her drone."

"Tell her not to worry. I have a feeling we'll have this case wrapped up in no time."

"Perfect. So are you on your way over?" Nans asked.

"I have to go and do some stuff at the bakery first, but what do you say to pick you up at noon?"

"That sounds perfect. Oh, and Lexy..."

"Yes?"

"Don't forget to bring some of those cupcake tops, and Helen wants a chocolate scone."

Lexy focused on her morning activities, baking several birthday cakes that had been ordered and the usual assortment of brownies, cookies, and bars for the bakery. When Cassie came to take over at eleven thirty, Lexy was anxious to get to Nans and follow up on the investigation. She boxed up the requested bakery items, bid Cassie a hasty farewell, and headed over to the retirement center.

"I thought you'd never get here," Nans said as she opened the door and ushered Lexy in. Ida was standing beside the door, eager to relieve her of the bakery box. She placed it on the table and then popped the top off and rummaged for a congo bar, which she wrapped into a big napkin and shoved into her purse.

"Come on, ladies, we don't have time to waste." Ida bustled over to the door, opened it, and exited into the hall without waiting for them.

"What's with her?" Lexy asked.

"Oh, Jason's been after her about the drone. He said it has a GPS tracker, and she's put some app on her phone that's supposed to track it. She's hoping she can home in on its exact location, so don't be surprised if she wants to go to the Pendletons' today," Helen said as she shoved a napkin-wrapped blueberry muffin into her purse.

"But first, we're going to Amelia Little's house." Nans took Lexy's elbow and ushered her toward the door.

They piled into the VW Beetle, and Lexy drove over to Amelia's while the ladies munched happily on their baked goods.

"On the way back, maybe we could swing by the Pendletons'," Ida hinted.

"That depends on what we find out. If we get a lead from Amelia's sister, we may have to go wherever that takes us," Nans said.

"And we need to swing by Susan's, too." Ruth patted her purse. "I glued the flap of her bank statement back so no one would know we tampered with it, and we really should get that back into her mailbox."

"I have to be back at the bakery at four," Lexy added. "You know, I do have a business to run— unless you ladies want to pay me for chauffeuring you around."

She peeked at them in the rearview mirror to see three furrowed brows.

"I can drive," Ruth said.

"Yeah, but we like to get there in one piece," Helen added as Lexy pulled up in front of Amelia's apartment building.

They hopped out of the car and marched up to the door. Nans knocked the same as she had the day before. The sister answered, her face softening as she recognized them.

"Oh, did you guys come back to talk to Amelia already?" the sister said.

"Yes. Is she back from her trip? How was it? I hear the weather was lovely," Ruth said.

The sister shrugged. "I wouldn't know. She got in late last night when I was asleep and had to go to work early this morning. She texted me that she had a good time, but she had early cleaning, so I haven't seen her."

The ladies exchanged raised-brow glances.

"But her luggage is here, right?" Nans asked.

"Yeah. Well, I think so." The sister looked at Nans funny. "You know you ladies are a little odd. What are you really after?"

"Like we said, we are from the paper and we're here to do an article," Ida huffed. Nans jabbed her in the ribs as the sister's frown deepened.

"I thought you were from the ladies' auxiliary, looking for a cleaner," the sister said.

"Yes, we are." Nans shot Ida a warning glare then leaned toward the sister. "Don't mind my friend here. She's got memory issues."

The sister's face turned sympathetic. "Oh, right. Well I don't know where Amelia is cleaning today, but you might come back later tonight. She had the early shift, so she should be out around four."

"Okay. We'll do that. Thank you very much." Nans turned away and walked down the porch.

"Early cleaning job my patootie," Ida said. "And I don't have memory issues."

"Are you sure, Ida?" Ruth said. "Because when we were here before, Mona told her we were from the ladies' auxiliary, looking for a cleaner. You almost blew our cover by saying we were from the paper."

Ida's cheeks reddened. "I'm sorry about that. I guess I'm just focused on finding this stupid drone."

"Don't worry, Ida, we'll find it. We know there's nothing wrong with your memory," Nans consoled her.

"So, do you think Amelia really had an early cleaning job, or did Rupert text the message to her sister?" Ruth opened the passenger door and slid into Lexy's back seat.

"If he killed her, he would probably have her phone. He could easily be sending texts to the sister, making it appear as if Amelia is alive," Helen said. "He might have even texted her about the trip in the first place."

"The sister said she left a note," Ruth said.

"Text. Note." Helen shrugged. "It's all the same to the young people these days."

"I wonder if we could contact the cleaning company and find out where she is or if she even came in today," Helen said.

"Maybe we could call up and pretend to be her sister looking for her." Ruth ventured a sly glance at Lexy. "One of us has a youthful voice."

"Yeah, but first can we swing by the Pendletons'?" Ida's eyes were glued to her smartphone, which was making pinging noises. "Jason put the screws to me about his drone, and I had to admit that I'd lost it. He sent me this GPS app, and I think I got it working. I think we can pinpoint the exact location."

"Really?" Ruth leaned across Helen to look at Ida's phone. "Is it that granular, though? How precise an area can it pinpoint?"

"I'm not sure. But at least we should give it a try. If we find the drone and the video, then we can hand this whole nasty business over to the police."

"Good point. That would sure be some solid evidence. But first, let's get this letter back into Susan's mailbox," Ruth said. "If the police start looking into things, it should be in there so they can find it."

"Good thinking. We'll go there first," Nans said. Lexy turned in the direction of Susan's house and parked in the empty driveway.

"She's not home," Helen said.

"Big surprise. She's probably still at the Pendletons' with Rupert," Ruth said.

"You'd think Olive would notice," Lexy said. "I mean, I'd notice if Jack was having an affair with someone that happened to be at our house all the time."

"Maybe they're really sneaky." Ida opened the mailbox for Ruth, who shoved the bank statement inside like it was a hot potato.

"Well, I'm glad to get rid of that." Ruth brushed her hands together and looked at Ida out of the corner of her eye. "We really shouldn't be tampering with the mail. If the police find out we did, they won't be able to use this as evidence."

Ida looked contrite. "I suppose you're right, but if I hadn't taken it, we wouldn't know that Susan was also being blackmailed."

"While we're here, we might as well take another look around," Helen said.

They scoured the perimeter of the house, looking into the garage, which was empty, and all the windows. Everything seemed pretty much the same as it had been the last time they were there.

"I don't know what we're looking to find," Nans said as they looked in Susan's bedroom window.

"Me either. Maybe some evidence of Rupert being here or the baseball bat or something...hey, her closet door is open. Was it like that before?" Helen asked.

"I think it was," Lexy said. "There's the shirt she wore in the photo that Rupert showed us from Paris. I distinctly remember that cute shirt with the daisies on it."

"So she has been back here since she came back from Europe." Nans' voice turned wistful. "I had half hoped she really was still in Europe, as she told her son."

"I know. Doesn't seem right, a mother lying to her son like that, does it?" Helen said.

"Well, when the mother is a murderer, lying comes easy," Ida said.

Nans sighed and turned away from the window. "I suppose so. I guess I was kind of rooting for them to still reconcile."

Ida snorted. "Well, they'll have to do that from jail then. Speaking of which, let's get a move on over to the Pendletons', and we'll see if I can locate the drone."

"Good idea. There's nothing new to see here," Helen said.

They were relatively quiet on the way over to Castle Heights, each with her own thoughts. Ida was busy fiddling around with her GPS app on her smartphone.

As Lexy turned onto the Pendletons' street, Ida blurted out, "We're getting warmer!"

"No kidding, Ida, we know the drone is on their property," Ruth said.

"Not necessarily," Ida said. "The dogs could have dragged it off anywhere."

"She does have a point." Nans pointed to a maroon Toyota Corolla that was parked in front of the Pendletons' house. "I wonder who that is."

"Maybe it's those fan club ladies," Ruth said.

"I don't know," Lexy said. "I got the impression they were a little more stealthy than parking right in front of the house."

Ida had already hopped out of the car and was pointing her phone like a Geiger counter at the front of the house. Sweeping it back and forth, she zoned in on one side and started walking forward.

They jogged up beside her.

"Are you zeroing in on it?" Ruth asked.

Ida pressed her lips together, her eyes flicking from the phone to the Pendletons' yard. "I'm not sure. It says it's over in this general direction, but I guess it's not very precise."

Ida kept walking toward the shrubbery and into the front yard.

Nans hesitated to follow. "Ida, I don't think we should just go traipsing through the yard."

"Why not? I think I got a bead on this thing." Ida started walking toward the front door. Nans hesitated, looked back at the rest of them, and shrugged.

Should they follow?

But just before they started to follow her, the front door opened.

A young blond woman backed out of the door. "I just wanted to thank you and let you know how much I appreciated the trip, even though I won't be working here anymore." The woman yelled as if the other person she was talking to was in another part of the house.

Nans turned to Lexy and mouth the word "Amelia?"

Nans hurried to the door. Amelia backed into her, almost sending the two of them tumbling down the steps.

"Oh, I'm so terribly sorry," Amelia said.

"Are you Amelia?" Nans asked.

The woman's brow furrowed. "Yes..."

"Well, it's lovely to meet you." Nans stuck her hand out. "I'm Mona. I've been looking for a cleaning lady, and I heard you worked here."

Amelia shot a glance into the house. "Well, I did, but..."

Ida had come up beside them. She glanced into the house too. The door was still open, and Lexy could see the foyer was rather grand, with marble floor and gold wallpaper. It was a little outdated, probably from the seventies, but still looked elegant. A credenza sat beside the door piled with mail. On the top was Olive's notebook. She recognized a robin's-egg-blue envelope. It was Connie's mail from the other day.

Ida must have recognized it too. She elbowed Nans out of the way and slipped into the foyer while Nans was talking to Amelia about cleaning.

"I do have next Wednesday in my schedule now, and..." Amelia saw Ida go in and cast a quizzical glance her way. "Hey, I don't think you should be in there." She looked back uncertainly at Nans.

"Oh, where are my manners?" Ida ran her fingers along the credenza. "I was just admiring this beautiful antique." Her slippery fingers grabbed the envelopes, sliding them behind her back and then into her purse.

Amelia must not have noticed Ida's sleight of hand. Nans had pulled her aside and was whispering in her ear. "I'm sorry. That's my dear friend Ida. She's senile."

Amelia looked sympathetic, and Nans pulled Ida out the door. "Ida, now, come along. We're not visiting here."

She pulled Ida down the steps, grabbing the card Amelia was now extending in her hand. "Thank you very much. I'll give you a call."

From inside the house, they heard Rupert yell, "Amelia, are you talking to someone out there?"

"It's just these ladies from the..."

But they didn't stick around to find out. They hightailed it across the street to Lexy's car and got out of there as fast as they could, Ida's search for the drone all but forgotten.

Twenty-Three

"Now I guess we know who the victim is," Nans said when they were seated at her dining room table twenty minutes later.

"It sure wasn't Amelia." Ruth took a bite of her chocolate-frosted brownie. "She looked pretty much alive to me."

"That's right. Rupert must have sent her off on vacation so that she wouldn't be around when he murdered Connie," Nans said.

"But why get rid of her now?" Lexy asked.

"He probably doesn't want anyone poking around in the house that could find any evidence as to what he's done."

Ida picked at her ham-and-cheese scone. "But that would mean that he doesn't intend to hire a new cleaning lady."

"Maybe he does, but just not yet." Ruth looked at them over the rim of her coffee cup. "Because maybe he's not done doing things that he doesn't want someone to see."

"You mean he's planning to do away with Olive?" Ida asked.

Ruth shrugged. "Well, her car is still missing. I took the liberty of peeking in the garage when you guys were fooling around at the front door and stealing mail. The red Cadillac isn't in there, only Rupert's truck and the sister's white Fiat."

"So the sister is still there? I wonder why Olive doesn't think it's odd that her sister's hanging around?" Lexy asked.

"Maybe her sister hangs around there a lot normally. Her son did say she spent a lot of time with Olive and Rupert. We don't know what the norm is for these people. Plus, we know the sister did go home at some point, since she mailed the letter, and we saw the shirt she wore on the trip to Paris in her closet," Nans said. "All we know for sure is that the sister went to Europe with Olive, she doesn't want to reconcile with the son, and she likes dogs. In fact, I think the little black dog we keep seeing at the Pendletons' is hers. Kingsley said she had a black one."

"The one we saw on the roof," Lexy said.

"Yeah. Imagine she put her own dog on the roof to lure Connie out," Ida tsked. "She can't be

200

that much of an animal lover if she put the dog in jeopardy that way. Not like her sister."

Nans went to the whiteboard and crossed off Amelia's name from under the "victims" category. "So now we know the victim wasn't Amelia."

"Which means it must have been Connie," Ruth said. "She was the blackmailer, and that's why they killed her."

"Makes sense. She would have been at the house a lot if she was Olive's assistant, so she might've seen some shenanigans," Helen said.

Ida opened her purse. "And I've got the proof right here." She produced the envelopes she'd taken from the credenza at the Pendletons' and fanned them out on the table in front of her.

Nans leaned over Lexy's shoulder to look at them. "Good work. One of those is Connie's bank statement."

Helen pushed up from her chair. "And I know just how to open it. I don't condone this type of behavior, but..." She snatched the envelope and hurried toward the kitchen.

"This is great, but how are we going to get Jack to investigate? We can't use the bank statement as evidence. We stole it from the Pendletons' house," Lexy said.

"We could pretend we got it out of Connie's mailbox," Ida suggested.

"That won't work either, because we shouldn't have taken it from there, much less steamed it open. Both of those acts would make it inadmissible," Lexy said.

"Well, we're just gonna have to find another way," Nans said. "Maybe we should focus on proving that Connie is missing."

"Olive will probably notice that pretty soon," Lexy said. "If she's her assistant, they probably talk quite frequently."

Ruth pursed her lips. "I'm not so sure about that. I once dated a writer, and after he'd finish a book, he would take a month-long break. Olive is releasing a new book next week. She may not have any duties for Connie to perform. She might not have occasion to talk to her for several weeks."

Nans picked a cupcake off the tray. "I wonder if that was all part of Rupert's plan. Why he chose this week to kill her. Knowing that Olive wouldn't even notice she was missing."

Nans peeled the paper off the cupcake and then sliced it into quarters, popping one whole quarter into her mouth. "But Olive went over to get Connie's mail. Won't she be expecting Connie to come and collect it?"

"Probably the best thing is to be able to prove to Jack somehow that Connie isn't where she is supposed to be," Ruth said. "What about that club, Lexy? Didn't they say that they kept track of where Olive was?"

"Yeah. They seemed like stalkers, though we haven't seen them there anytime we've been there, so they must not be very dedicated ones," Lexy said.

"They can't be there twenty-four hours a day. If only they were, they might've seen the murder," Nans joked.

"Hey, maybe one of them saw my drone," Ida said.

"Maybe I can find something of interest on the fan page." Ruth pulled out her iPad and started typing, squinting down at the page, using her fingers to pinch the posts so that they would be larger and easier to read. Ruth's face scrunched up. "Well, this can't be right."

"What's that?" Nans craned her neck to look at the iPad.

Ruth turned it around so they could all see. It was an article about Murder-Con with a picture of a blond woman who looked similar to Olive, though the scarf partially obscuring her face and the giant sunglasses made it impossible to tell if it was Olive or Connie.

"Isn't Murder-Con the conference that's going on right now that Olive said Connie was at?" Lexy asked.

"Yes, it is." Nans scraped some frosting off another section of the cupcake with her fork. "If Olive is here in town and Connie is dead, then *who* is this?"

"Beats me. I thought maybe neither one of them was at the conference, but this picture was taken yesterday, and it says the fan club ladies are going to step up their efforts to figure out who it really is." Ruth squinted down at the iPad. "Seems like it's sort of a mission of theirs to figure out if the sightings are really Olive or Connie. Apparently they know Connie stands in for her."

"Well then, maybe they'll be able to figure out who it is and come up with some clues for us," Nans said.

Ruth turned the iPad around, showing a full-face picture of a blonde who had a similar hairstyle to Olive's and looked to be the same size. "That's Connie."

"She doesn't look that much like Olive," Ida said.

"The sister looks more like her. Maybe she should have had *her* stand in," Lexy said.

"Maybe she does! Maybe that's who is at Murder-Con," Ruth suggested.

"Susan could be pretending to be Connie to hide the fact from Olive that Connie is dead!" Nans said. "Maybe she even took the red Cadillac.

We should check if Olive let Connie take that when she was filling in as her."

"You mean Susan could have been pretending to be Connie who was pretending to be Olive?" Ida shook her head. "This is getting complicated."

"I'll say." Helen stood in the doorway, the bank statement dangling from her hand.

"What is it?" Nans asked.

Helen put the statement on the table. "According to this statement, Connie didn't have any big deposits."

"What?" Lexy leaned over to read the statement. It looked like a regular bank statement from someone who didn't have a ton of money. Similar to her own. "This doesn't look like she's been getting money from Rupert and Susan. I mean, she was getting tens of thousands. Wouldn't she have deposited some of it?"

"Maybe she didn't want a record of it. But where has she been putting it?" Ida asked.

"Well, maybe she's just been stashing it away under her mattress or something," Nans said. "You know, maybe she doesn't want to make it obvious that she's getting a large sum of money. Going to save it for later or dole it out a little bit at a time."

"But Rupert was getting bank checks. Wouldn't she have to cash those within a certain number of days?" Lexy asked.

"I think so. Probably ninety days." Ruth said. "Maybe she was using the cashier's checks to buy something. Jewelry, household items. Laundering the money, so to speak. Then she could return the items or sell them on eBay. Are there any eBay statements in your pile of mail, Ida?"

"I don't think so." Ida thumbed through the pile of mail like a deck of cards, and a single piece of paper fluttered up from the pile, landing upside down on the table.

"What's that?" Nans asked.

"I don't know. Doesn't look like mail. Maybe the grocery list." Ida flipped it over, and the room fell silent as they all stared at it.

It was a note on white-lined paper, handwritten with a black felt-tip pen.

Keep your mouth shut or you'll be next.

"Does that mean what I think it means?" Helen asked.

"Yep. Looks like a threat to me," Ruth said.

"But what was it doing in Connie's mail?" Lexy asked.

Nans shook her head. "No, that wasn't in *Connie's* mail. That was on the credenza with Olive's notebook. That note wasn't for Connie. It was for Olive."

Everyone's head swiveled toward Nans. "You mean Rupert wrote Olive a threatening note?"

Nan spread her hands. "It's the only explanation. Olive lives in the house and is in a position to be able to find evidence of the murder. Maybe she's been asking questions and Rupert is trying this one thing to keep her quiet."

"He's probably just trying to get her to keep her mouth shut long enough for him to execute his plan to kill her," Ruth said.

"Well, if that's true, we don't have much time. We need to tell Jack," Ida said.

"Tell Jack *what*?" Nans asked. "Connie's bank statement showed no deposits, so we have no evidence to show that she was blackmailing them. We have no body. No murder weapon. Heck, we don't even have a motive. And without any of those, what can Jack possibly do?"

"She's right. We don't have any evidence to give Jack right now, but we do have something." Ida held her phone out with the GPS app open. "I think I figured out how to get this thing to be even more precise, and if that's the case, I should be able to locate the drone."

"And on the drone is all the evidence we need," Ruth said.

"In that case, we have but one choice," Nans said. "Tonight under the cover of darkness, we must go to the Pendletons' and retrieve the drone."

Twenty-Four

Lexy wouldn't lie to Jack, so it was a good thing he was working the night shift that night and, technically, she didn't have to lie because he didn't even know she was going out. His rule of not talking on the phone and only texting when he was on the job was working in her favor. Otherwise he might've called and asked what she was doing. The fact that he was working was good for another reason too. If they got arrested he'd be able to keep them out of jail. Hopefully.

Lexy dressed in all black. Black jeans. Black T-shirt. She was contemplating her black hoodie, but it was too hot out. When she arrived at the retirement center, Nans, Ruth, Ida, and Helen were waiting for her at the door, also dressed in black, except instead of jeans and T-shirts, they wore identical black polyester pantsuits accessorized with gigantic black patent-leather purses. Ruth was holding her wetsuit.

"You're not going to need that, are you?" Lexy pointed to the wetsuit. She didn't relish the idea of recovering a body that had been underwater for over a week.

"I figured if we can't find the drone, maybe we could dig up the body."

Lexy glanced up at Nans, who shrugged. Better to just put the wetsuit in and argue about it later.

They got in the car, and Lexy headed toward the Pendletons'.

"Okay now, we need to make this a stealth operation," Nans said. "Ida, you need to keep your phone shielded so that the light can't be seen from the house. We don't know if Rupert will be home."

"Check," Ida said.

"And we all need to be quiet. No talking. We'll use the owl signaling system," Nans continued.

Lexy slid her eyes over to Nans. "Owl signaling system?"

Nans frowned at her. "Don't you listen to anything I tell you? That's the stealth system we use for communication. One hoot to indicate things are going fine, two hoots to indicate you found something, and three hoots to indicate get the heck out."

"Oh, right." Lexy vaguely remembered Nans explaining the system to her before. She hadn't paid much attention, not expecting to ever be going on a covert operation at eleven p.m. with her grandmother and her three senior-citizen friends.

"Cut the lights! Cut the lights!" Nans whispered sharply as Lexy turned onto the Pendletons' street.

"What? I won't be able to see if I turn off the lights," Lexy said.

"You can coast," Ruth said. "If you leave the lights on, Rupert might see us coming."

Lexy pulled over to the side and turned off the lights then inched the car slowly forward. She didn't want to park right in front of the Pendleton house, so she pulled up three houses down.

The street was quiet, and most of the houses' windows were dark. Several of them had outdoor lights on. Cars sat cold in the driveways. A few parked on the street in front of the houses. It appeared that the entire neighborhood was asleep. They sat in the car, waiting for a few minutes. Nothing moved in the neighborhood, and the air was silent except the occasional peep of a frog or chirp of a cricket.

"Okay, I think the coast is clear." Nans popped her door open slowly and quietly. "Ready?"

The four old ladies slipped out of the car as silent as ninjas. They shuffled down the street, keeping to the shadows of the hedges and shrubs that dotted the yards. They slipped into the Pendletons' yard virtually undetected.

"Hoot," Ruth said.

"Hoot," Nans answered.

Ida pulled out her phone, shielding the screen with her hand.

"*Ping!*"

"Ida, turn that down!" Nans whispered.

Ida pressed a button on the side of the phone then continued looking at the shielded display in her hand. "This way," she whispered, nodding toward the back corner of the Pendletons' yard where the half-built gazebo stood.

They walked slowly across the yard, sticking to the shadows. Lexy's nerves were on edge, expecting the dogs to come racing and barking and the lights to blare on at any minute. Her phone vibrated in her pocket, and she took it out, shielding it with her palm as Ida had done with her phone. It was a text from Jack. She didn't dare not answer it lest he suspect she was up to something.

Olive Pendleton's car found at Lakeside Garage. Getting a new fan belt.

Hmmm... That was odd. Apparently their theory of Rupert taking the car to some desolate place to fake a disappearance or Susan taking it to the conference had been off. She was only getting a new fan belt. Lexy refrained from telling Nans and the others. The less talking they did the better. It could wait.

They slowly followed Ida as she veered first to the east and then to the west, heading toward the gazebo in a serpentine pattern.

"It's over there." Ida pointed toward the gazebo.

"In the gazebo?" Helen whispered.

"I suppose there's lots of places for the dogs to hide it," Lexy said, remembering how Sprinkles loved to hide things under other objects or dig holes in the ground.

"I saw them digging under that wood pile when we were here before. Maybe it's there," Ida said.

They moved up even with the gazebo, and now Lexy could see how slipshod the building of it was. Had Rupert only started the project so he could have the excuse of having cement around? Her eyes had adjusted fully to the dark, and she scanned the area for the blue tarp, remembering how Jack had said Rupert could have wrapped the body in it and weighed the whole package down. The blue tarp was nowhere to be seen.

Ida waved her phone back and forth as if it were a dowsing rod.

"It says it's over there, but..." She nodded toward the side of the gazebo, where Lexy could see they'd set up a little area for cooking out.

"Looks like they're moving their outdoor kitchen up here," Lexy whispered.

"Seems odd to me," Nans said. "Construction isn't even finished. And look at this weird foundation." Nans pointed to the foundation, where forms had been set up that looked a lot deeper than they needed to be.

"Maybe he needed a deep footing because it's muddy here," Helen said.

"I don't think this GPS tracker is working," Ida whispered. "It seems to think the drone is in—"

A light snapped on, illuminating them and freezing them in their tracks, and then they heard Rupert's voice. "I'm getting a little sick of you old biddies nosing around here."

"Hoot hoot hoot," Ruth yelled.

"Yeah, it's a little too late for that, Ruth." Ida hid her hand with the phone behind her back and puckered her face into a look of confusion. "Snooping? Why, I thought this was my bedroom? Isn't this the way to my room?" Ida looked from Nans to Ruth to Helen innocently.

"We're very sorry, Mr. Pendleton," Nans said. "My friend here wandered out of the retirement facility. She sleepwalks and gets confused easily. We had to follow her over here."

Rupert's brows mashed together. "You don't think I'm going to buy that, do you?"

"Why? You know she's not all there."

"Why are you people really here?"

Nans' eyes flicked from Rupert to the pile of lumber. She sidled toward it. "Okay, let's cut the malarkey. I think you know why we're here."

"No, honestly. I have no idea. What is it that you want? An autograph? A signed book? Pictures to put in one of those tabloid papers?"

Ruth scoffed. "Still playing, I see? We'll have you know that *we* know what you're up to. Where's Susan? I thought she'd be right behind you."

Rupert looked confused. "Susan? She's in Europe."

Helen laughed. "Yeah, sure she is. We know she's here. Her car is in your garage."

"Yeah, she left it there when she went to Europe with Olive. They took it to the airport and left it in long-term parking. Then when Olive came back by herself, she drove it back. Susan is staying on."

"I think you can stop pretending now," Lexy said. "We know what you're up to. We know what you've used the cement for, and we know what's in your pond."

"You ladies are *all* senile. You're bat-shoot crazy like that fan club. I want you off my property. Now." Rupert waved the flashlight toward the front of the house. Lexy and Nans exchanged a confused look. Was he going to let them get away?

Ida was over by the freezer with her cell phone out in plain sight now. It appeared as if she was homing in on the location of the drone.

"Not a chance, buddy. We know what you've done, and the proof is right in here." Ida tapped the top of the chest freezer.

"What are you talking about? Oh no, don't open that!" Rupert looked worried. Scared, even. "Olive is doing an experiment for her new book, and if you open the freezer, it'll ruin—"

But Ida didn't follow directions so well. She whipped the top of the freezer open triumphantly. Lexy expected her to produce the drone, but instead her face crumpled, and she said, "Uh oh."

"What?" Lexy ran to her, her heart seizing when she looked inside the freezer. Nestled in the blue tarp was Ida's drone. Next to that, the baseball bat. But those two things weren't what caught her attention. The thing that caught her attention was what the tarp was partially wrapped around. A body. *Susan's* body.

Rupert hadn't murdered Connie—he'd murdered Susan.

***

"You wrecked the experiment!" Rupert cried.

"Experiment? Is that what you call this?" Nans said.

"My drone! It's frozen!" Ida had pulled the controller out of her purse and was pushing the levers back and forth. The drone inside the freezer didn't budge. "I'm not reaching in and getting it. You get it, Lexy."

Nans whirled on Rupert. "You won't get away with this. We have evidence now."

"What in the world are you talking about?" Rupert glanced back at the house nervously. "You've screwed up Olive's experiment, and I'm going to be in trouble for it. You ladies have ruined everything!"

He lunged toward Nans, who deftly sidestepped.

Ruth picked up a piece of lumber that was lying on the ground and swung at Rupert. She missed, clocked the side of the freezer, and fell down, sliding in the mud.

Rupert made another attempt at Nans, which she averted, and then he turned his attention on Lexy. She had the drone in her hand and her back

217

up against the freezer. He came at her, his hands reaching toward her throat. And then he stopped short. Looking down into the freezer, his eyes grew wide in horror just as the drone came to life in Lexy's hands.

"Let go!" Ida cried as she worked the controls.

Lexy loosened her grip on the drone, and it flew up into the air then plummeted, smashing into Rupert's head. He fell to the ground and lay there, knocked out cold.

"We've got him!" Nans cried.

"Hoot! Hoot!" Helen said.

"And I've got the evidence." Lexy held up the USB card she'd taken from the drone.

"But I don't understand what actually happened now," Nans said as they all stood around, looking at Rupert's inert body. "Susan was the victim, not Connie. But why?"

"That does screw up our theory for the motive, now, doesn't it?" Helen said.

"Unfortunately, a lot of our evidence doesn't make much sense now."

"Why would Rupert want Susan dead?"

"Oh well, that's not a problem anymore. We've got the killer. We've got the evidence. We can hand it over to the police. Lexy, why don't you call Jack and—"

Click!

"Not so fast, ladies. Throw down your phones and step to the back of the gazebo."

Twenty-Five

Olive Pendleton stood at the opening to the gazebo, pointing a shiny black gun at them.

"It's okay, Olive." Helen waved her hand at Rupert. "We've got him immobilized. You're safe."

"You think Rupert is the killer?" Olive laughed. "He's not man enough to kill anyone. Or smart enough. He never even suspected that the reason I sent him to the farthest store for cement was so I could have enough time to kill Susan and drag her into the freezer. He thought I was all sweaty because I was washing the patio. Had to to get rid of the blood, of course."

"You killed your own sister?" Nans' eyes flicked from Olive to the freezer.

"I had to. I couldn't risk not living in the manner to which I've become accustomed. And Rupert..." Olive looked down at her husband with disgust. "Well, he couldn't provide for me if his life depended on it. Just like Momma and Daddy always said."

"But why?" Ida asked. "I don't get it."

"Figures you wouldn't. I noticed you're a little slow on the uptake. I also noticed you ladies have been sniffing around where you don't belong. Which is why I had Rupert make the foundation for the gazebo big enough to fit six. Though it looks like I'll have to stick Rupert in there now too."

Lexy's eyes jerked to the foundation. That's what had looked so strange about it. Olive had had Rupert make it large enough to stick a body in the concrete. Lexy had been so sure that Rupert had been using the concrete to weigh the body down in the pond when this whole time it had been Olive who had wanted the concrete to make a foundation to bury the body in. No wonder they'd been fooled by Olive's lack of concern about draining the pond. She didn't care if anyone messed around in there because the body wasn't stashed there.

But what could they do now? She glanced over at Ida. Was Ida going to knock Olive out with the drone like she'd done to Rupert? Ida was pushing and pulling at the controls, but the drone lay dormant. It must have been damaged by the assault on Rupert. It lay there useless no matter how much Ida fiddled with the controls.

"You! The senile one. What are you doing with that gizmo?" Olive gestured to Ida with her gun. "Put that thing down."

Ida looked conflicted, but she placed the controller down at her feet and muttered, "Stupid thing wasn't working anymore anyway."

Olive glanced at the drone. "Oh, so you're the ones that belong to that thing. Well, now no one will be able to use whatever it has on it as evidence, because it's going into the cement along with the bat and your bodies."

Panic fluttered in Lexy's chest. They had no weapon, and Olive had every incentive to kill them. In fact, there was no way she could let them live. She knew they owned the drone and...well... they'd seen the body that she'd admitted to killing.

Lexy wondered how she'd gotten the drone in the first place. Had she seen it buzzing around? More likely the dogs had brought it to her. Had she wondered all this time if someone had witnessed the murder through the drone's camera, and did she have any idea there was a video of it sitting on the USB card in Lexy's hand?

Nans had always told her that if they got into a bad situation, the best thing to do in front of the killer was to stall for time by keeping them talking. Maybe she could distract Olive with the conversation while she worked her way over to the nail gun lying on the other side of the gazebo.

"I still don't get it," Lexy said. "Aren't you going to get a lot of money from your new book that comes out next week?"

"Pffft! Hardly. My publisher takes most of that. And as you can see"—Olive gestured back toward the dilapidated house—"I'm in need of funds."

"But what about the money you inherited from your parents?" Nans asked. "I thought they were quite well off."

"*They* were. But ten years is a long time, and I have to live to a certain standard. Not to mention that Rupert has very expensive tastes."

"But Susan doesn't have expensive tastes. Susan invested her money and saved it, didn't she?" Lexy asked, taking a tentative step toward the nail gun.

"That's right. Little Susan, the pretty one. Oh, everyone always fawned over her. She was so pretty, and I was supposed to be the ugly, smart one." Olive snorted. "Well, it turns out I really *was* the smart one."

"So you killed her for her share of the money," Ida said.

"That's right. She had plenty. Even more than what my parents left us. And that son of hers was coming around, and she wanted to reconcile with him!" Olive got a sour look on her face, and Lexy took the opportunity to sidle closer to the tools.

"And if they reconciled, she would have put him back in the will, wouldn't she?" Helen asked.

"Yes. And I couldn't have that happen. I'd worked very hard the last few years to get Susan to put *me* in as the beneficiary. Not to mention I'd worked long and hard to get her to give us money for the various projects we need to do here. If that no-good Brent came here, I'm sure he'd put a stop to that in no time. He only wanted her money, and he wouldn't want her spending it on me."

"Susan never went to Europe, did she?" Ruth asked, drawing Olive's attention and allowing Lexy to move closer to the nail gun.

"That's right. Aren't you the smart one."

"But *you* were in Paris," Ruth continued. "You took a selfie with the paper showing the date and later on photoshopped your sister in to make it look like she was there."

"I have other talents aside from being an author, you know."

"That's why the same shirt was in her closet. It was an old picture. She never wore that shirt in Paris. You cropped her out of some other picture.

She drove over here that Saturday, and you killed her. That's why her car is in the garage. Then *you* went to Paris alone," Lexy said.

"Well done. That's correct, and since my car is in the shop, it was very convenient for me to just use Susan's," Olive said. "After all, she wouldn't be needing it."

"And her dog," Lexy said. "The little black one. You put him on the roof."

Olive looked apologetic. "Now, I never put that dog in harm's way. He was perfectly safe up there in the valley of the roof. I had him secured up there, but not so that Susan could notice. And now I have him here as part of my brood. I love him as much as my own dogs."

"So you answered the letter to her son, pretending to be her. You told him you didn't want to reconcile and were taking an extended trip to Europe." Helen's eyes turned sad. "You did all that so he wouldn't come here and try to talk to her in person, didn't you?"

Olive nodded. "Pretty clever, don't you think? I even had Rupert stick the letter in Susan's mailbox so that the postmark would be from her zip code. That was just a little trick I learned from one of my books."

Lexy chanced a sideways glance. Six more feet and she'd be able to lunge for the nail gun. They had to keep Olive talking.

"And that's why you sent Amelia on vacation," Lexy said.

"The maid? Yes. I did like her cleaning, actually. Even used to give her my older clothes. But she was very observant. I couldn't have her around to pick up on anything that was out of the ordinary. At least not until I'd taken care of Susan." Olive gestured toward the freezer.

"So when you had that pamphlet at Connie's the other day, that wasn't really from Rupert, then?" Ruth asked.

"No, of course not. I was giving it *to* Rupert. I told him that Amelia's cleaning was not sufficient anymore. He would have to find someone new. Of course, I didn't plan on approving of anyone, but Rupert didn't know that." She looked down at him, giving Lexy the opportunity to take another step toward the nail gun. "He was obedient in that way. I always knew I could count on him to run little things over to Connie. Too bad I'm going to have to do away with him now too."

"Yeah, Mrs. Jenkins said she saw Rupert going over to Connie's quite a bit," Helen said.

"Oh, that busybody," Olive made a face. "I wish I had a spot for her in the foundation, but it's getting quite crowded as it is."

Ruth tilted her head and looked at Olive inquisitively. "There's one more thing, though. The threatening note that said 'you'd better keep quiet or you'll be next'. Did you write that to Connie?"

Olive's brows shot up. "How did you know about that?"

Ruth shrugged. "We have our ways."

"Well, I suppose I could tell you, since you won't be around to tell anyone else. As a matter fact, I did write that to Connie. She'd asked about Susan's car in the garage and her dog being here one too many times, and I knew she was getting suspicious. So I wrote her that note. I was going to slip it under her door the day I ran into you busybodies at her house. But I couldn't very well do that with you people watching."

"Susan borrowed your sweater because she was frail and often cold." Lexy remembered Kingsley's words about Susan. It made sense that she might have borrowed it even if the day was warm.

"She was always borrowing my things. I'm glad that at least..." Olive glanced into the freezer, her face looking almost regretful. Did she have a pang of grief about missing her sister, or was her heart as frozen as Susan's body?

"Okay, well, here's what I don't get," Ida said.

Lexy took another step toward the nail gun while Olive's attention was on Ida.

Ida continued, "Susan had several large withdrawals from her bank account this past month. We thought she was being blackmailed, but now I assume that money was going to you, wasn't it?"

Olive's brows shot up. "Well, aren't you the little detective. What are you guys, some kind of amateur sleuths?"

Nan straightened her spine. "I'll have you know we are a bona fide private investigative service. The Brook Ridge Falls Ladies Detective Club."

"Well, excuse me if I don't ask for your card. You're not going to be around long enough for me to use your services. It's too bad things had to end this way. I could have used your knowledge for my books."

"Dang," Ida said.

Helen shot a look at her then turned back to Olive. "If you would just answer this one question for us since we are of an inquisitive nature, we'll go to our concrete graves with no struggle." Helen shot a look at Lexy. Apparently she was onto Lexy's plan about the nail gun and wanted to keep

Olive occupied for her so she could get closer. "Rupert got cashier's checks every other Tuesday. Where did he get the money for those, and what were they for?"

"Susan was always the sympathetic sap. I'd tell her about how my publisher pays me peanuts, and she'd have sympathy and give me money. I asked to borrow some money until my book release. That's what those withdrawals were. She was withdrawing money for me. But I didn't want to just deposit it because I didn't want the police looking into that later on. I didn't want to have anything that would look suspicious or tie me to her financially. Nor did I want her pesky son to figure out what was really going on in case he came back looking for her. So I had Rupert turn them into cashier's checks. Then later on I would use them to buy things to fix up the house or get some new shoes or purses."

"So Susan was giving you her money all along because you'd already spent all of yours," Nans said.

"That's right. She had plenty and I had nothing!"

"So you dipped into what she had, and even though she was generous with it, you still killed her," Ruth added.

"I couldn't let Brent come back and screw things up! Anyway, it's none of your business. Enough of this idle chitchat. Get over there and meet your final resting place!" Olive jerked the gun in the direction of the foundation.

"Now hold on, Olive. We can work something out," Nans held her hand out toward the gun, but Olive wasn't going to hand it over that easily.

She pointed the gun right at Nans' head. "I said get over there." She jerked the gun again, and the ladies shuffled toward the foundation.

It was now or never.

Lexy lunged for the nail gun.

"Hoot! Hoot! Hoot!" Nans, Ruth, Ida, and Helen yelled in unison.

Olive swung around in time to see Lexy pick up the nail gun and aim.

"*Bang!*"

White-hot pain seared Lexy's arm. The nail gun clattered to the ground unfired.

Lexy's energy drained as if someone had pulled a plug. She fell to her knees, her vision closing in on her.

In the distance, she heard a pack of dogs barking.

She slumped the rest of the way to the patio, her senses fading out just as she heard a strange rat-a-tat-tat.

Lexy struggled to stay conscious, her eyesight clearing just long enough to see Olive's scowling face looming above her before she toppled onto the pavers beside Lexy.

Twenty-Six

"Lexy! Talk to me!" Nans' voice sounded like it was a mile away. Lexy's head was fuzzy, and her arm stung like the time she'd been attacked by hornets that were nesting in her old metal swing set. Her cheeks felt like someone was rubbing warm, wet sandpaper on them.

Slowly she opened her eyes. She was on the ground, looking up at the lattice corners of the half-built gazebo wall at the trees above.

The gazebo!

She sat up quickly then fell back against someone who had been cradling her in her lap. "What happened?"

"Lexy! You're alive!" Ruth, Ida and Helen rushed over, clucking about like mother hens. Four furry dogs wiggled around her, licking her face and hands and jumping into her lap.

Then Lexy remembered she'd been shot! Her head jerked to the side to inspect her arm. Nans was pressing a napkin against it—apparently one she'd used to wrap up the last scone, since the scone was now lying on the ground. Her arm didn't look too bad. At least it was still attached.

"You were just grazed." Nans answered her unspoken question. "You'll be fine."

But she must not have been fine, because she was seeing double. She wasn't seeing just four gray-haired old ladies in black polyester pantsuits in the gazebo. She was seeing eight of them.

Was she seeing double? No, not *exactly* double, because Nans, Ruth, Ida, and Helen were crouched down next to her and the other polyester suits were tying Olive up with thick rope.

Lexy pushed to a sitting position, feeling much better now. "What's going on?"

One of the other suits turned to look at her, and Lexy recognized her as the woman from the fan club who had come into her bakery.

"We got here just in the nick of time," the woman said.

"Oh, Lexy, this is June, Sally, Belinda, and Florence. The women who run Olive's fan club."

"Olive's former fan club now." Sally scowled down at Olive's unconscious body.

"After Olive shot you, these lovely women rushed in, and Florence grabbed the nail gun and shot Olive right in the knees," Nans said.

"It must be really painful, because she passed out, and she's been out ever since," Ida added.

"If it wasn't for these ladies, we might be in our concrete graves right now." Ruth glanced over at the cement foundation.

"It's very much appreciated," Lexy said truthfully. She alternated patting first one dog then the next as they vied for her attention, seemingly unconcerned about their unconscious owners lying just feet away. "But what were you guys doing out here in the middle of the night?"

"Well, as you know, as part of our duties as fan club founders, we need to keep up on the comings and goings of Olive," Sally said.

"There is a big conference going on right now, and there is some question as to whether Olive herself is there or if she sent her assistant Connie to impersonate her," June added.

"So we were just doing a little midnight reconnaissance to see if we could spot her," Belinda said.

Florence leaned toward them and whispered, "You know she can be very reclusive."

"Anyway," Sally continued, "we were parked down the street when we saw you pull up. We wanted to see what you were up to, thinking maybe you were part of a rival fan club gang. We debated coming onto the property, but then we saw Olive come out of the house, and as we crept closer, we heard the conversation."

"So you heard her confessing to everything then?" Lexy asked.

"Yes, we did. And when she shot you, I don't know what came over me. I ran in, grabbed the nail gun, and shot her back."

"It was all very exciting," Belinda said. "Almost like being in our own mystery book."

"But that still doesn't explain what exactly *you* people are doing here," Sally said.

"We're private investigators," Nans said proudly. "We witnessed the murder with this drone here, and we've been investigating it ever since."

"Oh, well, we barely noticed you in those black outfits," Florence said.

"I noticed yours are very similar." Ruth went to stand beside Florence as they compared their outfits. "I got mine at Marshall's. Where did you get yours?"

"I got mine there too. They were on sale last month."

"I got mine at the same sale!"

The sound of sirens split the air, and they all looked at each other. "We should probably call the police."

"You haven't called them?" Lexy asked.

"No, we were more concerned with finding out if you were okay and securing Olive and then... well...we got to talking, and..." Nans shrugged.

"We figured we had the perpetrators well tied up anyway, so we had plenty of time." Ida cocked her ear toward the street. "And if my guess is right, the police are coming here right now anyway."

Ida's guess was right. The siren stopped outside the Pendletons'. The police came cautiously around back, saw them in the gazebo, and used their high-powered flashlights to light the place up like the nighttime field at the Super Bowl. Lexy squinted into the bright lights, her gut clenching when she heard Jack's voice.

"What's going on back here? We had a call about a disturbance...dogs barking and...Lexy, is that you?"

Jack rushed to her side, fussing over her wound, calling an ambulance against her wishes, then admonishing her for putting herself in danger.

"But we caught the killer." Ida pointed to Olive and Rupert.

"I see, but why is Olive tied up?" Jack asked.

"Olive was the killer," Florence cut in.

Jack whirled around, his eyes darting among Nans, Ruth, Ida, and Helen and the four ladies of the fan club. He zoomed in on the fan club ladies, his brows drawn together. "And exactly who are you?"

The woman stuck her hand out. "I'm Florence Dayton, president of the Olive Pendleton fan club."

"Former Olive Pendleton fan club," Sally reminded her.

"Yes, right. We don't want to have a fan club for a murderer," Florence said.

"So Rupert wasn't the killer?" Jack asked.

"No, and here's your proof." Ida held out the USB card from the drone, keeping the drone itself securely under her arm. Lexy figured she didn't want to let it get into police custody, as they would likely keep it in the evidence room for years, and she needed to get it back to her grandson. "On this card is the video that will prove who the killer is."

"And the body is right in the freezer," Nans said.

Jack nodded to one of the other police officers, who opened the freezer then turned back to Jack. "Yep, she's not kidding about that."

The ambulances pulled up just as Rupert was coming to. Jack made sure Lexy got loaded in the first ambulance before putting Olive and Rupert into their own separate ambulances. Then he climbed into the back of the ambulance with her.

"You don't have to come with me," Lexy said. "I'm fine. You have a job to do here."

Nans, Ruth, Ida, and Helen as well as the fan club hovered around the back of the ambulance, too.

"I'll go with her," Nans said.

"Give me your keys, Lexy, and I'll take the car and meet you guys at the hospital," Ruth said.

"I don't think that's a good idea." Lexy looked nervously from Ruth to Jack.

"I'll meet them at the hospital," Jack said. Then, realizing the ladies probably didn't have a ride, he added, "I'll drive you all there."

"Well, that's settled, then." Ruth started toward Lexy's car but stopped when Caspian Kingsley appeared in a royal-blue bathrobe with gold fleur-de-lis on it.

"My word. What *is* going on over here? I only called because the dogs were making a ruckus. This seems like quite a to-do."

"That's right, Mr. Kingsley. In case you don't know, there was a murder here. And our town's most famous author is being charged with it," Florence said.

Caspian looked her up and down. Then his gaze flitted from Florence to the other fan club ladies and then over to the sleuths. A flicker of recognition crossed his eyes when he looked at Nans, Ruth, Ida, and Helen.

"My Lord, there's eight of them?" He looked at Jack then leaned in toward him as if providing him a confidence. "I don't know what happened here, but I wouldn't put any stock in what these ladies say. From what I've seen, they're all crazy."

Twenty-Seven

Lexy sat at one of the café tables in the front of her bakery the next day and watched the sun glinting off the waterfall across the street. Pedestrians strolled casually down the road, clutching shopping bags. Birds skittered around on the sidewalk, looking for crumbs. No one would guess a murder had occurred nearby and someone had been arrested for it just the night before.

She picked up the cinnamon scone in front of her, wincing at the pain in her right arm where the bullet had grazed her. She'd have to learn to use her left arm for a while. Cassie came out from the kitchen to load a fresh batch of blonde brownies into the pastry case.

"I can do that," Lexy said.

"No way. You are to rest. You're lucky I'm even letting you in here today. Jack would have my hide if he knew I let you do any work." Cassie's gaze drifted out the window. "And besides, you've got company."

Lexy turned to see Ruth's enormous antique blue Oldsmobile careening down the road. The driver pulled to the side of the street, misjudging how far to go, and its whitewall tires jumped up onto the curb. Then she overcorrected into the opposite lane, which thankfully was void of traffic. Finally she managed to park without running anyone over, and the four ladies piled out and made a beeline for the bakery.

Nans was the first through the door. "Lexy! You're looking chipper!"

The ladies had stayed with her for four hours in the emergency room. It had turned out the bullet hadn't done any damage, simply grazing the skin. She'd barely needed a couple of stitches. But Jack and the ladies had stayed by her side the whole time.

Ruth, Ida, and Helen followed Nans over to Lexy's side and inspected her arm. Once they were satisfied that she was okay, they did an about-face and marched to the bakery case, where they each picked out a pastry before filling up coffee mugs at the self-serve station.

"Now don't fill up too much on these, Ida," Nans said. "You know we're having the fan club ladies over for tea later this afternoon."

"You are?" Lexy asked. "You mean the ladies that helped us catch Olive?"

Nans nodded as she squirted some lemon into her tea. "Yes. They seemed very nice and it was the least we could do seeing as they got us out of quite a pickle."

"I just hope they don't think they can team up with us." Ida made a face.

"That's not going to happen," Nans said. "There's only room for four of us in the detective club... well and Lexy, of course."

"Of course," the ladies said in unison.

"Though we may be able to use them as informants somehow," Nans said.

"They seemed quite eager to work with us, and Sally does have extensive computer skills," Ruth added.

"And they are going to help with those adorable little Peekapoos," Helen said.

"They are?" Lexy asked. "What about Rupert?"

"Oh, he's keeping them. He said he wouldn't part with them. But he's going to need some help, and they agreed to help him." Ida leaned forward. "I think they might be sweet on him."

"So what's going to happen to Rupert, anyway?" Helen asked. "He's not being charged with anything, is he?"

"No. From what Jack said, he had no idea about the murder. It was all Olive's doing. They were able to prove with the video from the drone that it was her hand that wielded the bat. And they also got some DNA from the bat itself. Should be an easy case."

"Imagine killing your own sister," Ruth said.

Helen shook her head. "But Jason got his drone back in good condition, right, Ida?"

Ida nodded. "He did. I pretended I had just dropped it under Mona's sofa. He doesn't need to know we flew halfway across town and got it involved in a murder. If he did, he might not let me play with his toys anymore."

Lexy laughed. "Jack also said that Rupert is probably going to stay in the house. Olive is going to need to come up with a lot of money for bail."

"What about her assistant?"

"Turns out she really was at that conference all along," Lexy said.

"But will Olive still inherit Susan's money?" Ruth asked. "That doesn't seem right since she killed her."

Nans shook her head. "She won't be able to inherit. But Rupert will."

"No he won't," Lexy said. "I mean, technically he will, but he said he planned to get in touch with Susan's son, Brent. She had confided in Rupert that she wanted to reconcile with Brent. Rupert had no idea Olive was intercepting the letters between them, and since he put that mail in the box for Olive, he feels a little responsible."

"So it sounds like Rupert really was a nice guy," Helen said.

"It seems so. At least he's doing the right thing. And he's going to make sure Brent gets all of Susan's money."

"Well, it seems like we tied up another case that the police couldn't solve." Nans held up her coffee cup. "I think that calls for a toast."

Lexy, Ruth, Ida, and Helen all raised their cups.

"To a job well done," Nans said.

They clinked the lips of their cups, and each took a sip.

Ida raised her cup again for another toast. "And here's hoping there's many more."

The End.

About Leighann Dobbs

USA Today Bestselling author Leighann Dobbs has had a passion for reading since she was old enough to hold a book, but she didn't put pen to paper until much later in life. After a twenty-year career as a software engineer with a few side trips into selling antiques and making jewelry, she realized you can't make a living reading books, so she tried her hand at writing them and discovered she had a passion for that, too! She lives in New Hampshire with her husband, Bruce, their trusty Chihuahua mix, Mojo, and beautiful rescue cat, Kitty.

Find out about her latest books and how to get discounts on them by signing up at:

http://www.leighanndobbs.com/newsletter

If you want to receive a text message alert on your cell phone for new releases, text COZYMYSTERY to 88202 (sorry, this only works for US cell phones!)

Connect with Leighann on Facebook:

https://www.facebook.com/leighanndobbsbooks

Also By Leighann Dobbs

COZY MYSTERIES

Blackmoore Sisters
Cozy Mystery Series

* * *

Dead Wrong

Dead & Buried

Dead Tide

Buried Secrets

Deadly Intentions

A Grave Mistake

Spell Found

Mooseamuck Island
Cozy Mystery Series

* * *

A Zen For Murder

A Crabby Killer

A Treacherous Treasure

Mystic Notch

Cat Cozy Mystery Series

* * *

Ghostly Paws

A Spirited Tail

A Mew To A Kill

Paws and Effect

Lexy Baker

Cozy Mystery Series

* * *

Lexy Baker Cozy Mystery Series Boxed Set Vol 1

(Books 1-4)

Or buy the books separately:

Killer Cupcakes

Dying For Danish

Murder, Money and Marzipan

3 Bodies and a Biscotti

Brownies, Bodies & Bad Guys

Bake, Battle & Roll

Wedded Blintz

Scones, Skulls & Scams

Ice Cream Murder

Mummified Meringues

Brutal Brulee (Novella)

———

Witches of Hawthorne Grove Series:

Something Magical (Book 1)

———

Regency Romance

***

The Unexpected Series:

An Unexpected Proposal

Dobbs Fancytales:

Dobbs Fancytales Boxed Set Collection

———

Western Historical Romance

***

Goldwater Creek Mail Order Brides:

Faith

American Mail Order Brides Series:

Chevonne: Bride of Oklahoma

———————

Contemporary Romance

***

Reluctant Romance

———

Sweetrock Cowboy Romance Series:

Some Like It Hot (Book 1)

Too Close For Comfort (Book 2)

————————